Dear

Dee

Temptation novel, *Jilt Trip*, as a jilted bride and a man who once—and still—had a thing for her, though he wasn't about to admit it. It's wonderful when characters of one book come alive and demand their own story the way these two did. They just didn't expect to be paired up.

As to where to set their story, Texas is my favorite setting, and in *Bedded Bliss*, you'll visit the coastal city of Galveston and the beautiful Hill Country. Although I've lived here many years, I'm not a native, but I'm the mother of native Texans—one of whom plays high school football—so I figure I'm in.

I hope you enjoy *Bedded Bliss* and the rest of the Greatest Texas Love Stories of All Time books.

Warmly,

Greatest Texas Love Stories of All Time

Heading to the Hitchin' Post
1. *Unforgettable Bride* by Annette Broadrick
2. *Precious Pretender* by Stella Bagwell
3. *Mail-Order Brood* by Arlene James
4. *A Willful Marriage* by Peggy Moreland
5. *Her Kind of Man* by Barbara McCauley
6. *Storming Paradise* by Mary McBride

He's a Cowboy!
7. *Christmas Kisses for a Dollar* by Laurie Paige
8. *Lone Wolf's Lady* by Beverly Barton
9. *Love, Honor and a Pregnant Bride* by Karen Rose Smith
10. *Some Kind of Hero* by Sandy Steen
11. *The Cowboy Takes a Lady* by Cindy Gerard
12. *The Outlaw and the City Slicker* by Debbi Rawlins

Lone Star Lullabies
13. *Texas Baby* by Joan Elliott Pickart
14. *Like Father, Like Son* by Elizabeth August
15. *Mike's Baby* by Mary Lynn Baxter
16. *Long Lost Husband* by Joleen Daniels
17. *Cowboy Cootchie-Coo* by Tina Leonard
18. *Daddy Was a Cowboy* by Jodi O'Donnell

Texas Tycoons
19. *The Water Baby* by Roz Denny Fox
20. *Too Many Bosses* by Jan Freed
21. *Two Brothers and a Bride* by Elizabeth Harbison
22. *Call Me* by Alison Kent
23. *One Ticket to Texas* by Jan Hudson
24. *His-and-Hers Family* by Bonnie K. Winn

Feisty Fillies
25. *A Girl's Best Friend* by Marie Ferrarella
26. *Bedded Bliss* by Heather MacAllister
27. *The Guardian's Bride* by Laurie Paige
28. *Millie and the Fugitive* by Liz Ireland
29. *My Baby, Your Child* by Nikki Benjamin
30. *Hannah's Hunks* by Bonnie Tucker

Trouble in Texas
31. *Guilty as Sin* by Cathy Gillen Thacker
32. *Family Ties* by Joanna Wayne
33. *Familiar Heart* by Caroline Burnes
34. *Double Vision* by Sheryl Lynn
35. *The Loner and the Lady* by Eileen Wilks
36. *Wild Innocence* by Ann Major

Men Most Wanted
37. *Lawman* by Laurie Grant
38. *Texas Lawman* by Ginger Chambers
39. *It Happened in Texas* by Darlene Graham
40. *Satan's Angel* by Kristin James
41. *The Lone Ranger* by Sharon De Vita
42. *Hide in Plain Sight* by Sara Orwig

Cuddlin' Kin
43. *West Texas Weddings* by Ginger Chambers
44. *A Mother for Jeffrey* by Patricia Kay
45. *Desperate* by Kay David
46. *Father in the Middle* by Phyllis Halldorson
47. *The Texas Touch* by Kate Thomas
48. *Child of Her Heart* by Arlene James

GREATEST TEXAS LOVE STORIES OF ALL TIME

BEDDED BLISS

Heather MacAllister

Feisty Fillies

HARLEQUIN®

TORONTO • NEW YORK • LONDON
AMSTERDAM • PARIS • SYDNEY • HAMBURG
STOCKHOLM • ATHENS • TOKYO • MILAN • MADRID
PRAGUE • WARSAW • BUDAPEST • AUCKLAND

HARLEQUIN BOOKS
225 Duncan Mill Road, Don Mills,
Ontario, Canada M3B 3K9

ISBN 0-373-65240-2

BEDDED BLISS

This edition published by arrangement with Harlequin Books S.A.

Visit us at www.eHarlequin.com

Printed in U.S.A.

HEATHER MACALLISTER

USA TODAY bestselling author Heather MacAllister lives in Texas and is married to her high school sweetheart, who challenged her to learn Morse code, get her ham radio license and he'd take her to the senior prom. Her license arrived in the mail the day of the prom.

A former music teacher, Heather might still be teaching if her sons hadn't kept running off baby-sitters. After taking pity on the child-care industry, she quit teaching and began avoiding housework by writing during her sons' naptime. Heather sold her first book to Harlequin Romance in December 1989. Since then, she's published thirty-five books with Harlequin Romance, Harlequin Temptation, continuity series and online with eHarlequin. Her award-winning romantic comedies have been translated into twenty-five languages and published in dozens of countries.

She won the Romance Writers of America Golden Heart Award, is a three-time RITA® Award finalist and won a *Romantic Times* magazine award for Best Harlequin Romance.

When she's not writing, Heather spends her time collecting vintage jewelry, directing a handbell choir, watching fireworks displays and killing plants. You can visit her online at www.HeatherMacAllister.com.

Books by Heather MacAllister

Harlequin Temptation

Jilt Trip #543
Bedded Bliss #583
Christmas Male #616
Bride Overboard #637
Long Southern Nights #656
Manhunting in Memphis #669
Mr. December #711
The Good, the Bad and the Cuddly #757
Moonlighting #785
Personal Relations #817
Tempted in Texas #864
Skirting the Issue #892

To Jeanette Bail

With fond memories of the Poulenc,
the Rachmaninoff and *Scaramouche.*

1

Dee Ann Karrenbrock was naked.

Completely, totally, unexpectedly naked. In spite of the pounding of her head and the roiling of her stomach, she should have recognized this fact immediately, but mistook the tangle of sheets for her usual cotton nightgown.

Now that she knew she was naked, the next step was to establish why. No, she thought, keeping her eyes and her mouth tightly closed, she didn't want to know why just yet.

At that moment, the room lurched and Dee Ann thought perhaps she should start with the question where—as in where was she? Swallowing dryly, she opened her eyes and was assaulted by walls painted a bright, unfamiliar yellow. Then she looked down and saw that the sheets wrapped around her were a garish black, yellow and white stripe.

She didn't recognize any of it.

Dee Ann closed her eyes again, this time listening for voices. She could hear a rhythmic ticking and a faint whooshing, but no distant conversations. And the room seemed to move.

I must have the flu. But this was the worst flu bug she'd

ever had. Shivering, she rolled to her side, pulling the sheets with her.

They slipped away and, annoyed, Dee Ann yanked.

Someone yanked back.

Dee Ann's eyes flew open. Slowly...gently...*discreetly,* she turned her head.

A broad expanse of male back reposed immediately to her left.

It was a lovely back. A prime back. A manly back. The lovely back of a man in his prime. Pure, unblemished skin with leanly defined muscles tapering into a taut waist and firm— Oh, Lord, he was also naked.

Dee Ann released the tension on the sheet and it whispered over the man's hips.

Who was he? Unfortunately, his head was buried under a pillow. Dee Ann mentally ran through the extremely short list of male backs she might reasonably expect to find in this situation. Currently, there weren't any. In fact, Dee Ann did not recognize this back at all.

There were no moles, scars or tattoos to give her a clue, either.

Concentrate, she commanded her throbbing head. The wedding. She'd attended Carter and Nikki Belden's wedding on a private Galveston beach. She'd stayed for the reception...toasted the bridal couple...

And that's all she could remember.

Dee Ann bit her lip to keep from moaning aloud. So much for who, what, when, where and how. As for why, she had only to look at the gorgeous back inches away from her to know why.

In spite of her efforts, a moan escaped.

The man didn't move and Dee Ann decided that this would be an excellent opportunity to determine his identity.

Clutching what little sheet she could to her chest, she eased toward him and lifted the side of the pillow. All she could see was a mass of dark hair. She tried to raise the pillow a bit higher, but the man's arm tightened on it as he mumbled in his sleep.

All right, she'd just go around to the other side of the bed. Scooting to the edge, she looked for her clothes. The black and yellow indoor-outdoor—who on earth decorated this room?—carpeting was bare. She leaned over to search beneath the bed, but it was built to the floor, as was the dresser next to it. No sign of her clothes anywhere.

Fighting a rising panic, Dee Ann crawled over to the man. Holding up the sheet with her teeth, she grabbed the pillow with both hands and jerked it away from his grasp.

"Hey!" He turned toward her, grimacing and drawing a hand to his temple.

"You?" Dee Ann screeched.

The sheet fell down.

She clutched the pillow to her chest and stared in horror at the man she'd shared a bed with.

"Ow," he moaned. "Give me back my pillow."

"No!"

"Please stop shouting," he whispered in the careful way of a person with a very bad headache. Without opening his eyes, he groped with his hands, found the sheet and drew it over his head.

He was not going to ignore her. Outraged, Dee Ann snatched the sheet and pulled it down. "What are you doing here?"

"I'm trying to die in peace." With obvious irritation, he stretched out his arm. "Give me my pillow." When she didn't comply, he opened his eyes and froze. *"Dee Ann?"*

She tightened her hold on the pillow.

"Oh, my—" Breaking off suddenly, he changed his expression and started to lever himself into a sitting position. Becoming aware of the arrangement of the sheets, he stopped, awkwardly supporting himself on an elbow. With a game smile, he cleared his throat. "Good morning."

"Not when I find myself in bed with Julian Wainright, it isn't."

He squinted at her through one eye. "Tsk-tsk. And here I thought we'd put all that ugliness about the stock swap—"

"Stock swindle," Dee Ann corrected. "You and your cohorts swindled me!"

"Now, Dee Ann, we offered you current market value. Could we help it if that was somewhat less than you'd paid?"

"Beast."

"You didn't have to accept our offer."

"I did if I wanted to save my grandmother's coffee shop!"

"Correct me if I'm wrong," Julian mused aloud, one finger to his lips, "but your grandmother is the one who sold it to us—making herself a tidy profit, I might add."

"She didn't know you were going to raze the place! I will never forgive you for that, Julian. Never."

Julian shrugged, rippling the sheet. "We were getting along so well last night, too."

"Last night..." She wished she could remember last night. "Last night was a terrible, hideous, horrible, awful, revolting, disgusting mistake!"

"It wasn't good for you?" he drawled, his voice still husky from sleep.

"Obviously not, since I can't remember a blessed thing," she snapped, irritated that he could look and sound sexy while she sounded like a shrew and probably looked worse.

"Thank God," Julian said with relief, collapsing onto his back.

"Why? Why thank God? What happened?" She fired the questions at him, dreading the answer.

He waved away her words. "I have absolutely no idea."

It must be really awful, then. Dee Ann sat back on her heels. "Yes, you do. You must."

"Why?"

"Because...because you're the man and I'm the woman."

"And I suppose that piece of irrational logic confirms it," he said.

"Don't patronize me. I can be as logical as any man."

Julian yawned. "I don't doubt your masculine reasoning capabilities, Dee Ann. I doubt your feminine ones."

Men always felt threatened by capable women, Dee

Ann thought. She had discovered this time after time in business. Julian, in particular, was insulting her because she'd once rejected him as a lover and had subsequently bested him in a business maneuver.

Of course, due to her father's sentimentality over her grandmother's coffee shop, Julian's side had ultimately prevailed, but they both knew Dee Ann had really won.

"Such a typical male reaction," she retorted. "Whenever a woman gets the better of a man, he attacks her feminine traits as if they were defects."

"You don't have any feminine traits."

Dee Ann threw the pillow in his face, so furious she forgot why she was clutching it to her chest in the first place.

Julian raised an eyebrow. "I stand corrected."

Mortified, Dee Ann grabbed the sheet, leaving Julian uncovered. Idly, he plopped the pillow over his waist.

Dee Ann concentrated on mummifying herself in the sheet, to Julian's silent amusement. "If you were half the gentleman you pretend to be, you'd leave the room so I could dress!"

"You are *not* a morning person, are you?" Julian leaned over the edge of the bed, duplicating Dee Ann's search for her clothes.

She hoped he'd have better luck. Apparently, he didn't. "Are my pants—"

"No."

"Hmm." He looked at her.

"What are you waiting for?" she demanded.

"The bathroom is behind you. In mere moments, I'm going to walk into it and grab a towel. If the sight of a male body offends you, perhaps you'll want to avert your eyes." He swung his legs over the side of the bed just as Dee Ann covered her eyes with her hands.

She heard a chuckle. "No peeking."

"I wouldn't."

"I certainly would," he said on his way around the bed.

He was taking his time, too, judging by the sound of his feet padding over that hideous carpet. "Last chance," he offered.

"Hurry *up!*"

"Aw, c'mon. Aren't you the teensiest bit curious? Assuming that you truly don't remember anything about our night of love."

"We did—not—have—a night of *love!*" She nearly bit off her tongue spitting out the words.

"But then, you don't know, do you? Perhaps the sight of me in all my manly glory would, er, jog your memory?"

She wanted to scream at him, but his suggestion did have merit. Not a lot, but her pounding head wasn't offering any alternate suggestions.

And a tiny part of Dee Ann—a very small part that she normally didn't listen to—*did* want to see if the rest of Julian was as gorgeous as his back. And his chest.

Not that she had any doubt that it wouldn't be. Julian took pride in his appearance and, frankly, had great material to work with.

She'd always thought Julian was attractive; she wouldn't have dated him last winter otherwise. Not that looks were the most important criteria in a relationship, but one couldn't ignore the father's contribution to his children's gene pool. Yes, Julian had some great genes to contribute. Unfortunately, he didn't want to contribute them anywhere. Dee Ann was seeking a husband and a father for her future children. Julian was an enthusiastic bachelor. And with her biological clock ticking away, Dee Ann didn't have time to waste.

"Going once...going twice..."

Dee Ann uncovered her eyes and mentally prepared to maintain a composed, clinical expression.

She opened her eyes and caught her breath.

Lounging against the doorway, Julian was wearing the most devilish grin she'd ever seen. His eyes, the parts that weren't bloodshot, gleamed.

He was also wearing a yellow towel knotted around his waist. "Made you look."

"You are despicable."

"And you need to lighten up." He straightened, no longer smiling.

"I see nothing to be light about," she grumbled. "I don't even know where we are."

"We're on the *Honey Bee,*" he said, walking across the cabin.

"The *Honey Bee?* The Beldens' *yacht?*"

Julian nodded as he pulled striped curtains away from a porthole. The line where sky met ocean wobbled like a defective horizontal hold on a television set.

That explained the moving sensation. She'd thought that the flu had affected her equilibrium.

Frowning, Julian peered outside a moment before

facing her. "Yes, this is the master stateroom on their boat."

"Why aren't *they* in the master stateroom?"

"Good question."

"Do you have a good answer?" she asked, not sure she wanted an answer at all.

"Nooo." Julian rubbed his forehead and squinted out the porthole again.

It made Dee Ann's stomach queasy just looking. "Do you think they're somewhere on the boat?" she asked, although she doubted the Beldens were anywhere around. They should be on their honeymoon. Here, on this boat.

She could tell by Julian's expression that he didn't think he'd find his friends, either. "I'll check and you can get dressed."

Tightening his towel, he strode from the cabin.

"But I don't know where my clothes are," Dee Ann said to the empty room.

Well, now was the time to find them.

Pulling the sheet from the bed, she headed for the tiny bathroom and found only towels. She was standing in the middle of the cabin wondering what to do next, when Julian returned.

"We're alone," he announced.

They held each other's gaze for several seconds before looking away.

"Um, were my clothes out there, perhaps?"

"Didn't see them." Julian seemed preoccupied.

"Did you find *your* clothes?"

"Nope."

"Oh." Dee Ann sank onto the bed and stared out the porthole. "What time is it?"

Julian gestured behind her. "According to the world's loudest timepiece, it's just after one o'clock."

"In the afternoon?"

"It would appear so."

This was...unbelievable, that's what it was. Dee Ann had never found herself in such a situation. Julian was being no help whatsoever, only staring at her with a brooding expression she couldn't interpret. Obviously, it was up to her to come up with a plan of action. So be it.

"Did you park your car at the dock?"

"I hope not. I shouldn't have driven in my condition. And I remember..." He smiled slightly. "I remember a lot of giggling and stumbling. I think we walked."

"I can't imagine doing it, but take a look outside. Maybe we threw our clothes on the dock." She *hoped* they'd thrown their clothes on the dock. "Well, go on," she urged Julian when he didn't move. "If our clothes are out there, we can get dressed and leave."

"Dee Ann—"

"Surely you don't expect *me* to go out there like this."

"Nobody can see anything with you in that sheet."

"All right then." She stood. Julian Wainright, however much he styled himself the gentleman, was not one. She, however much recent events might suggest otherwise, was a lady.

Holding her head high, she swept past him as though she were attired in a gown from the finest couturier.

"Dee Ann, we aren't at the dock."

Not at the dock? "Well, where are we?"

He pointed out the porthole. "Anything look familiar?"

"There's nothing out there but water!"

"As far as the eye can see," he said.

"You mean, we're out in the middle of the Gulf of Mexico?"

"I hope not the middle, but yes, I do remember being in the pilothouse with you. And we started the motor."

"I remember that!" Thank heavens, she recalled *something*. "And you let me drive!"

"Is that all you remember?" Julian crossed his arms over his chest.

"No...I remember the lights from the oil rigs and how pretty they looked." And she remembered something else. "You kissed me!"

"And you kissed me back."

Unthinkingly, Dee Ann brought her fingers to her lips, reliving the feel of Julian's kisses. As with everything he did, Julian kissed with style.

And such style. With Julian, kissing became a sensual exploration rather than something to be hurried through as a prelude to "the good stuff," as one early date had informed her.

Dee Ann sighed. At least she had the memory of Julian's kisses.

She just wished she could remember everything else.

The bed was the only place to sit, so Dee Ann returned to it.

"Does your head ache as much as mine does?" Julian asked.

"I thought I had the flu. Maybe it's food poisoning, if you've got it, too."

He sent her an incredulous look. "Dee Ann...we got rip-roaring drunk. Snockered. Sloshed. Smashed."

"Maybe *you* did, but I do not get drunk."

"You sure did last night."

"Why are you being so insulting?" Her voice quivered and she knew she was near tears, but at this point, she didn't care.

Suddenly, Julian's demeanor underwent a radical change. "Dee Ann, don't cry. Crying women give me hives. Uh, there's a first-aid kit in the galley." He climbed through the companionway. "I'll look for some aspirin."

Dee Ann allowed her tears to spill over and dribble down her cheeks.

Drunk. He thought she'd been so vulgar as to get drunk. And if Julian thought she was drunk, then everyone else at the wedding must have thought so, as well.

Now they were all talking about her and she knew exactly what they were saying. *Poor Dee Ann Karrenbrock. Look at her. Obviously still in love with Carter Belden. He jilted her, you know. Right at the altar. They said he was ill, but here it is less than two months later and he's remarrying his ex-wife. It was so brave of Dee Ann to come today, but look at her, the poor girl. Drunk as a skunk.*

She covered her face with her hands and surrendered to the tears. The thing was, she honestly wished Carter and Nikki well. She liked Nikki, when she'd never expected to. And Nikki felt the same way. They'd marveled at the fact that they might actually become friends, even though Nikki had ruined Dee Ann's wedding. Nikki was smart and strong and had great business ideas. Dee Ann enjoyed their conversations.

As for Carter, Dee Ann was fond of him and felt she would have made him a good wife.

But she hadn't loved him and he hadn't loved her.

She was never going to find anybody to love.

Nobody was ever going to love her.

She sobbed harder.

"Take this, you'll feel better." She felt the mattress shift as Julian sat beside her.

Sniffing, Dee Ann took the aspirin and washed it down with the glass of water Julian had also brought. "Thanks," she said, handing the glass back to him.

Dee Ann tried hard to stop crying, but a sob escaped as she wiped her eyes with the end of the sheet. "I don't like to cry."

"Come here," Julian murmured and took her in his arms.

Dee Ann couldn't resist. For a man who got hives from crying women, he knew exactly the right thing to do—nothing. He simply held her as the storm of her weeping passed, then stroked her back in soothing circles.

"I'm sorry," Dee Ann apologized when she could. "I know you hate this." *And me.*

"Try not to be so hard on yourself. You made a mistake. It's done."

"But you don't understand," she said, pushing herself out of his arms. "I didn't even finish my second glass of champagne."

"You didn't lose count?"

"No. Don't you remember, I got all congested because of the roses?"

"I know you're allergic to them." Julian's eyebrows drew together. "But we were outside on the beach."

"It must have happened when I was inside the tent for the ceremony." Dee Ann thought back. "Anyway, I stopped drinking the champagne and ate some shrimp and cheese. I would have left, but..." She finished with a shrug.

"You didn't want people to talk." Julian ran a hand through his hair, which responded by falling into place.

Dee Ann tentatively touched her own hair. Her French twist had become untwisted long ago, and she could feel a fine grit coating the sticky strands. Ugh.

"You didn't eat or drink anything else?" Julian asked.

Dee Ann shook her head. "No, because I took an antihistamine and switched to the lemonade."

Julian's eyes widened. "What lemonade?"

"You know, the pitchers the caterers had stashed in the serving tent?"

"By the bar?"

Dee Ann nodded. "They had pitchers of pink lemonade. I guess they were saving it for later. I poured myself a glass and took my pill."

"How many glasses?" Julian asked sharply.

"One. I'm not a pig. Wait a minute." She touched his arm. "That's when I began to feel strange! It got so hot,

I had another glass...I don't remember much after that."

Julian took her hand, which Dee Ann thought was a sweet gesture until she realized he was taking her pulse. "How do you feel now?"

"Lousy."

"Just lousy, or I'm-going-to-keel-over lousy?"

She pulled her hand away. "I'll survive."

He looked relieved. "Well, that explains what happened to you. You didn't drink lemonade—you drank hurricanes. Unlit hurricanes."

"I beg your pardon?"

"Haven't you ever been to New Orleans? A hurricane is a drink. High-proof alcohol is floated on top and lit. It was the grand finale to the reception. After dark, the waiters paraded around with these flaming drinks. Of course, a lot of that alcohol burns off. You got the straight stuff."

Dee Ann gasped.

"I'm surprised you didn't pass out," Julian said.

"So I *was* drunk!"

"Yes, ma'am."

Dee Ann punched him in the arm. "You seduced a drunk woman!"

Julian grimaced. "Please. I'm not going to argue with you until after I've had coffee. You want some?"

"I'd prefer tea, please. Decaf, if possible," she requested primly.

"Decaf?" With a look of disgust, Julian stood. "What's the point? Can't you just drink half a cup? How can you ruin a perfectly civilized drink that way?"

"At least I'm not dependent on caffeine to make me civil in the mornings."

Julian held up his hand. "Dee Ann, I think you're a very attractive woman. And I obviously thought so last night, too. But you have stated, and I'm inclined to agree with you, that last night was a mistake."

"It certainly was!"

"Fine. Let's agree to forget the entire episode."

Dee Ann felt better at once. She even managed a smile. "I think that's best."

They shook hands, very civilly.

"Now, let's go make our respective morning beverages, even though it's afternoon," Julian said.

Dee Ann followed him into the galley. The interior of the *Honey Bee* was impressively large. This was one expensive boat and, uneasily, Dee Ann wondered again where the Beldens were.

"May I help?" she asked Julian, showing him that she could be gracious.

"Yes. Cups, silverware and napkins are in there." He pointed to a tiny cabinet next to the fold-down table in the dinette.

"You seem to know your way around," Dee Ann commented.

Julian spoke over the sound of running water. "I've been on the *Honey Bee* before. Lots of times. Nikki and Carter owned it together when they were married to each other the first time and Nikki bought his share after the divorce."

Dee Ann squatted awkwardly in her sheet, but managed to find two yellow cups. She was beginning to hate yellow. She rose, and turning to the dinette table, she pushed aside a piece of blue paper, returning to it when she thought she saw her name.

She had. Dropping the spoons, she twirled the paper around and gasped. "Julian!"

"What is it?" He was beside her in two steps.

Mutely, Dee Ann pointed to her name on the paper. And Julian's name. And the scripted title, entwined with doves, ribbons and hearts.

"It's a marriage license," she whispered. "*Our* marriage license."

2

"LET ME SEE THAT." Julian ran his finger down the paper until he reached the bottom. He stared at it for an endless moment before showing her the scrawled signature. "It says here the ceremony was performed yesterday." Dee Ann snatched the license from Julian.

"By all means." But instead of moving away, as she wished he would, Julian stood shoulder-to-bare-shoulder with her and examined the paper.

Just under the illegible scrawl occupying the space allocated for the officiating member of the clergy or justice of the peace, was a legible date. She had married Julian Wainright sometime last night.

Dee Ann stared. She concentrated. She blinked, but the date remained and the memory didn't.

She *couldn't* have forgotten her own wedding! And what responsible person would perform a ceremony when the bride, and apparently the groom, as well, were...indisposed? The license must be a fake. Someone's idea of a joke. Someone who would want to torment her. Who? Who would be so cruel?

Studying the blue paper, Dee Ann noticed that while her name was typed, Julian's wasn't. She'd seen this wedding license before, but not since a certain day in June. "This is *my* wedding license," she said, feeling equally disgusted and humiliated. "The one for my wedding with Carter. Someone has blotted out his name and written in yours." Her hands trembled and she dropped the paper. "Is this your idea of a sick joke?"

"You surely can't think *I* had anything to do with this!" An unaccustomed pallor marred Julian's face.

That, more than anything he could have said, convinced Dee Ann he was telling the truth. "Who else?"

"I can think of lots of people—"

"Oh! How...horrid!" She backed away from him.

"Dee Ann...I didn't mean that the way it sounded."

"Just how *did* you mean it?"

"Only that in celebrating such a joyous occasion, people's spirits run high and, after a few drinks, perhaps their judgment was somewhat impaired." He smiled thinly. "As ours was."

Dee Ann had felt a pang when Julian referred to the Belden wedding as a "joyous occasion." Were people *that* relieved Carter hadn't married her? "Perhaps your judgment was impaired, Julian, but at least my behavior can be attributed to mixing drugs with alcohol."

There was a short silence. "I *see.*"

It was only as Julian's eyes widened that Dee Ann realized what she'd said. "An *antihistamine!* I took an antihistamine with what I thought was lemonade. You, though, what's your excuse?"

"Bob," he said with a groan and a shake of his head.

"Bob?" Dee Ann drew a blank, something that was occurring with distressing frequency lately. "Are you by chance referring to Robert Smith, the Karrenbrock Ventures comptroller?"

Julian held his head still. "Yes. Bob the Traitor."

"Oh, please." Dee Ann gave a little trill of laughter. She knew she'd done it well when Julian's eyes narrowed ever so slightly. A sore point. Good. "People change jobs all the time and no one thinks of them as traitors." She shrugged. "He made a shrewd career move."

Julian crossed his arms and leaned against the counter connecting to the galley. "And a whopping profit at our expense."

At her expense, as well, but Dee Ann chose not to remind Julian of that. "You Belden people are so despotic."

"You hired him out from under us!"

"You would have fired him as soon as you found out he sold us his shares of Belden stock," Dee Ann retorted.

"Exactly." Julian reached around her and picked up the license. "He was a traitor. He can be bought and we know his price. Comforting thought, isn't it?" he murmured before glancing over the license and tossing it back onto the table.

"Robert made a smart career move," she repeated. "That's the only thought I have on the subject." Dee Ann tightened the knot on her sheet. "And I find it rather petty of you to blame him for your drunkenness."

For a moment, Dee Ann thought she'd gone too far, but Julian, with only the tense set of his jaw to betray him, merely looked toward the galley. "I believe your water is boiling."

He didn't offer to make her tea, Dee Ann noticed, though he did gesture for her to precede him into the tiny space. She ignored the blue paper on the dinette table and took one of the mugs with her into the galley.

There was no decaffeinated tea and what tea she found was in bags. The Beldens obviously weren't tea drinkers or they would have stocked loose tea. Dee Ann made do by dunking the tea bag briefly in the water.

"Lemon?" inquired Julian in an impersonal voice.

"Oh, *is* there?" The world would be a much better place if Dee Ann could have lemon in her tea.

Opening the minirefrigerator, Julian handed her a yellow plastic ball with a green screw cap.

Dee Ann closed her eyes against the horror. The Beldens were barbarians. Nevertheless, it was slightly better than nothing. She accepted the plastic lemon without comment.

In the end, she had to strengthen the tea to mask the odd taste of reconstituted lemon juice of an indeterminate age.

Julian drank his coffee and watched her, the brooding expression on his face once more. "You're fussy, aren't you?"

Dee Ann swept past him and sat at the dinette table. "If by fussy you mean I adhere to certain standards, then yes, I suppose I'm fussy."

Julian greeted this speech with a crack of laughter. Very unlike Julian. "And you sit there wearing a sheet!"

Dee Ann straightened her shoulders. "To you it may

appear to be a sheet, but I assure you that right now this—" she looked down at herself "—is a sarong."

Julian snorted. "Then you slept in your clothes."

Dee Ann set down her mug so hard that tea sloshed out and wet the corner of the wedding license. "Why are you being so mean to me?"

"Because I don't appreciate being treated like the bad guy," he said, gesturing with his mug. "You have absolved yourself of any blame or responsibility."

"At least I didn't try to blame everything on poor Bob!"

"*He's* the one who got me drunk!"

Irate, Julian stood before her, wrapped only in a towel.

Dee Ann's attention was captured by the rise and fall of his bare chest and the smoothly defined muscles of his abdomen. Taut and lean, that was Julian, she thought with unwilling approval. No ostentatious muscular bulges to spoil the lines of his suits.

She contrasted Julian's torso with that of the considerably shorter, potbellied Bob. "What did he do—sit on you and force you to drink?"

"No." Abruptly, Julian took the seat across from her.

Each carefully avoided looking at the wedding license, though Julian slid it away from the puddle of tea. "Bob has begun making his own wine. He brought a case of it to the wedding and insisted I sample each variety and pronounce judgment."

"You see? You're considered an expert and he values your opinion. You should be flattered."

Julian sent her a sour look over his coffee mug. "The wine's not ready to drink. Too raw."

"You obviously were able to choke some down."

"What was I supposed to do?" he asked, exasperated. "Take a mouthful, swish it around and spit it at his feet?"

"Perhaps you could have compromised between normal wine-tasting protocol and guzzling who knows how many bottles," Dee Ann responded primly.

Julian sighed, closed his eyes and drained his coffee. "My head aches. That stuff of Bob's packed a wallop."

"How much did you drink?"

"Enough for him to feel good and me to feel bad."

"Quite noble of you."

Slowly, Julian opened his eyes. "Yes, actually, it was."

Dee Ann met his look. "Too bad that nobility didn't extend to me."

This time, she *had* gone too far, but she hadn't been able to stop herself. What was the matter with her? Why did she keep sniping at Julian? She was in a dangerous position to be antagonizing anyone, especially the only other human being for miles around.

Julian's gray eyes had turned icy with dislike. He hated her, but she'd known that ever since she'd caught his expression across the Belden Industries conference table during her failed attempt at a takeover.

The thing was, he *had* been civil since then. They'd all been terribly civil, which was no doubt the result of Nikki's influence.

But it went deeper with Julian. He'd never forgiven

her for choosing Carter over him. Dee Ann admitted to herself that she'd handled that badly, but Julian dated widely and nonexclusively. Among her circle of acquaintances, it was understood that Julian was not seeking a life partner. Dee Ann, however, was. So though they'd gone out twice, she'd had no idea that he felt anything stronger for her than attraction.

Unfortunately, she knew that whatever attraction he'd once felt, last night notwithstanding, was over.

This last realization was confirmed with Julian's next words. Plucking a dry corner of the marriage license, he held up the certificate. "You know what this really says about you, Dee Ann? It says that a man has to be drunk to marry you."

"No, it says that I had to be drunk to marry *you!*" He'd found her most vulnerable spot. Her deepest fear was that she never *would* find a man to marry and father her children. Time was running out. She was already thirty-one and had embarked on serious husband-hunting three years ago. The shallow pool of candidates was drying up. This fiasco so soon after Carter's jilting would destroy her social reputation in Galveston.

Galveston? Who was she kidding? She might as well cross every bachelor in the entire state of Texas off her list.

She could see it all now. In little black books everywhere, there would be an asterisk by her name with the notation: Avoid. Desperate for husband and children.

But she would rather die a spinster than reveal any of this to Julian. With a look of complete contempt, she sipped her tea.

And burned her tongue. Her eyes teared. *Great. He probably thinks I'm crying again. Maybe I should.*

"Give it up, Dee Ann. You're so desperate to get married that you carry around a fill-in-the-blanks wedding license."

"I don't!"

Julian jiggled the paper. "Here's the evidence."

"Evidence? *Evidence?*" She snatched the paper from him. "I'll show you evidence." Grabbing the bottom of her sheet sarong, Dee Ann clambered up the steps to the deck.

"Where are you going?" Julian called after her.

She didn't answer.

Dee Ann couldn't remember ever being angrier in her life. Not even when Julian and the others had ruined her wedding to Carter by luring him away as she was walking down the aisle with her father. But that anger couldn't touch the fury she felt now.

She wasn't *that* desperate for a husband and she didn't want him thinking she was. Dee Ann's teeth chattered, she was so mad. She raced to the railing and ripped the wedding license into as many pieces as she could, then flung them overboard.

The dramatic gesture was spoiled when the wind carried some of the pieces back on deck, plastering others against the side of the *Honey Bee.*

"Dee Ann!" Julian caught up with her in time to witness blue confetti raining onto the deck.

"There! Instant divorce!" she snarled and whirled. She stepped on the hem of her sheet and tripped, but caught herself before she fell, waving off Julian's arm.

"Leave me alone! You wouldn't want me to think you cared or anything."

Spying a square of blue dancing across the deck, Dee Ann snatched at it, then at another.

"What are you doing?" Julian asked.

"I'm destroying evidence." Two more squares; it looked at though as much of the paper had blown back on board as out to sea.

The sheet was getting in her way. Dee Ann hoisted the hem over her arm and marched to the railing, conscious of Julian's amused regard. She didn't care.

As Dee Ann raised her arm, a memory flashed. She hesitated, then tossed the pieces into the ocean. Something seemed terribly familiar. She'd done this before. Recently.

"No!" Covering her mouth with her hands, Dee Ann turned to Julian in horror. "I remember!"

"What?"

"I...we..." She pointed to the ocean.

"*What?*" Julian stared from the ocean to her.

"Maybe it was a dream. I remember standing here and...and..." She gestured mutely.

Realization dawned and Julian slowly walked to the brass railing. "That was no dream."

"You mean, I really threw my clothes overboard?" Dee Ann wailed.

"You threw mine overboard, too."

"No!"

"Oh, yes."

"Oh, God." Dee Ann's legs gave way and she sat on

the nearest hunk of metal. "What could I have been thinking?"

Julian cleared his throat. "I believe the word *prude* may have come up in the conversation and you were demonstrating how it didn't apply to you."

"Of course it applies to me!"

Julian smiled. "Not last night."

Something about the tone of his voice made Dee Ann narrow her eyes. "You're remembering things, aren't you?"

"Mmm."

He didn't elaborate and Dee Ann wasn't sure she wanted him to.

This was quite possibly the worst day of her life.

Julian leaned on the railing and faced the ocean. He looked unperturbed, or more likely, lost in memories. The breeze ruffled his hair attractively. Even his beard stubble added to his good looks, shading his jaw with interesting hollows.

The breeze also caught the edge of his towel and flapped it open. From where she sat, Dee Ann saw nothing, but imagined plenty.

Might as well add sex-starved to the spinster designation she would no doubt carry with her to her grave.

Another piece of the ubiquitous wedding license scampered past her feet as if mocking Dee Ann's thoughts. As she bent down to get it, the wind carried it underneath where she was sitting. She knelt on the deck and reached between the metal box and the side of the boat.

"What are you doing?" Julian asked.

"More evidence."

"Dee Ann..."

She heard him sigh, then he joined her. "Don't worry about it. I think you've been sufficiently thorough."

Not until every *trace* of last night was erased. She stood and walked around the box. "It's caught under this metal thing."

"Let me help you." Julian walked around and stopped.

When he didn't move, Dee Ann looked up at him questioningly.

"That's the anchor," he said. "It's caught under the anchor."

He seemed very shaken by the fact.

Dee Ann stood. "It's okay, Julian. I doubt it's hurting anything."

"It's not okay."

"It was just a tiny piece—"

"Dee Ann, it's under the *anchor*."

"Is that bad?"

He muttered something unintelligible. "Ask yourself why the anchor is on deck instead of in the water." Julian let that sink in for a moment, then headed for the pilothouse.

"We're adrift," Dee Ann whispered to herself. "Julian? Are we adrift?" She trotted after him.

"It appears so," he answered before ducking into the pilothouse.

It might be the hottest part of the day, but Dee Ann felt a chill. "Where are we?" she asked as she stepped into the small enclosed area housing the boat's navigating instruments.

"How should I know?" Julian snapped.

"You might try reading these instruments." Dee Ann pointed to a likely-looking one which had been blinking a changing set of blue numbers.

"One forty-seven dot four three five," Julian rattled off and looked at her.

"Well?" she asked. "What does that mean?"

"I have absolutely no clue."

He didn't? "Don't joke. I'm not in the mood."

Julian drew a deep breath and looked skyward. "I'm not joking," he said, exhaling.

As they stared at each other, Dee Ann heard the slapping of the waves and the pounding of her heart. "What do we do now?"

"Look for some maps or charts or whatever they're called," Julian ordered.

Dee Ann was too alarmed to take offense at his tone. "Do you know how to read those?"

He shot her a dark look. "No, do you?"

"No."

"Then I guess we'll learn together, won't we?" he said with a brittle smile.

Dee Ann felt light-headed. "Don't you know anything about boats?"

"Very little," Julian admitted, fiddling with the radio.

"But I thought you said you'd been on the *Honey Bee* before. *Many times*, in fact."

Julian glared over his shoulder. "You've ridden in airplanes, do you know how to fly them?"

He had a point. Dee Ann looked for maps. She found them, rolled up in tubes. "I think these are what you want," she said. "They're labeled."

"Find one that says Gulf of Mexico."

But wouldn't that map already be out? Dee Ann picked through them, her fingers cold. "Eastern Gulf, Western Gulf, Florida Gulf..."

"Try Texas Gulf."

There was no Texas Gulf. There was, however, a book lying next to the radio. Gingerly, Dee Ann reached across Julian and tapped it.

Without so much as a thank-you, Julian grabbed the book and flipped through the pages. "Dee Ann," he said, his voice unnaturally cordial, "perhaps you could check the library and see if there are any instruction manuals or how-to books?"

"You mean, like *Boating for Beginners?*"

He glanced at her. "Unless you find a copy of *Hints for the Naked Adrift at Sea.*"

"Very funny." Dee Ann climbed the steps. "At least we aren't in an airplane and have to worry about crashing."

"No," Julian said, squinting from the book to the instruments. "But we can always run into something and sink."

Visions of being stranded on a desert island with Julian sent Dee Ann scurrying across the deck, her sheet swishing behind her.

Once below deck, Dee Ann decided that her first priority was finding something else to wear. Maybe Nikki kept clothes on board, though they didn't wear the same size. Dee Ann was several inches taller and, she thought with satisfaction, several inches larger in certain strategic areas.

Unfortunately, one of those strategic areas proved to be her hips, Dee Ann discovered. None of the shorts she found in the master-bedroom bureau would zip. Was there to be no end to her humiliation?

No, she discovered after trying on a couple of swimsuit bottoms.

She had given up, when a wad of yellow, black and white stripes caught her eye.

"Oh, Nikki, how...precious." Dee Ann held up swimsuit bottoms made out of the ghastly stripe used all over the *Honey Bee*. The woman had had a suit made out of the same fabric. Had she no taste whatsoever?

As she laughed to herself, feeling superior to Nikki once more, Dee Ann became gradually aware that the suit appeared to be bigger than the others. She stretched her hands apart.

"Well, no wonder. The elastic is shot." And then something occurred to her. A stray thought she tried to push away.

"No. I'd rather..." Be what? Naked? She was.

What if Julian couldn't figure out what to do and where to do it before they sank? Just what would be her chances of swimming ashore wrapped in a sheet? She'd lose the sheet and then she'd have nothing.

With resignation, Dee Ann stepped into the suit bottom. It fit, of course, except that it left a large area south of her navel exposed.

She dug in the drawer and located the swimsuit top

and a pair of trunks. Grinning, she tossed them on the bed. If she had to wear this stupid suit, then so should Julian.

The thought of Julian appearing in bee upholstery cheered Dee Ann enormously. It almost made up for the sight of herself after she fastened the top.

Even the limp elastic didn't give enough to prevent Dee Ann from overflowing the cups.

She looked obscene. Cheap. Trampy.

"*Very* nice," drawled a voice from the doorway.

Dee Ann whirled away from the mirror, her hand ineffectively covering her bounteous cleavage.

"This is a new look for you, isn't it?" Julian advanced into the room.

Dee Ann retreated, matching him step for step. "At least this is better than being wrapped in a sheet."

"Definitely."

"You're drooling, Julian."

He grinned, still walking toward her. "Tell me again why we hate each other?"

"I don't hate you." Dee Ann backed into the bed and lost her balance.

"Better and better," Julian murmured, his eyes following the bounce of Dee Ann's breasts.

She felt mortified...and strangely excited at the same time. To her recollection, no man had ever looked at her with such unvarnished and unapologetic lust.

Desire and respect, yes. She knew she was attractive and dressed herself with classic elegance. It usually appealed to the sort of man who was, himself, classically elegant. A man like—

"Julian!"

He'd sat next to her and moved close—too close.

"Yes?" he whispered, just before kissing the side of her neck.

She jerked away. "What are you doing?"

"I'm kissing you." He captured her chin and held it steady while he kissed the side of her jaw, then underneath it and went on to her collarbone. She knew where he was headed.

"Julian." She wiggled away. "Why?"

"Because you look so...lush." He drew back and gazed into her eyes.

Dee Ann's jaw grew slack.

Never breaking eye contact, Julian leisurely drew his finger from her chin, tracing a path down her neck and pausing in the hollow of her throat where her pulse beat wildly, betraying her.

His lips curved in a satisfied smile.

Dee Ann swallowed and her breathing quickened. She couldn't move, mesmerized by the intensity of Julian's gaze.

Slowly, his finger continued its downward course until he reached the valley between her breasts. Only then did he look down. Turning his hand over, he grazed his knuckles across the tops, following the curves exposed by the suit, then lowered his arm and met her eyes once more.

Dee Ann expected to feel outrage. Instead, something uncoiled deep within her. "You...touched me," she breathed, more to herself than Julian.

He responded with a whisper. "Why don't you touch me?"

It was a dare and an invitation at the same time and Dee Ann was still under his spell. Without hesitation, she raised her fingers to his jaw, feeling the roughness and the corresponding tingling in her fingers. Then she traced the outline of his ear. Julian had perfect ears.

He covered her hand with his, placed a kiss in the palm then held it in place on his chest.

His heart thumped at a feverish pace nearly matching her own. Fascinated, Dee Ann lingered there until she felt his pulse slow.

She looked up at him and saw him watching her from heavy-lidded eyes. Shifting her weight, she brought her other hand to his chest and skimmed both over the smooth skin, exploring the texture, watching Julian's expression.

Responding to an impulse formed deep within her, Dee Ann lowered her mouth and kissed a trail across his chest.

Julian gasped softly. "Dee Ann..." Cupping her face in his hands, he met her eyes with a question in his.

She never got the opportunity to answer.

"Ahoy, *Honey Bee!*" sounded a loud tinny voice.

They sprang apart. "What was that?" Dee Ann squealed, clutching Julian's arm.

"Listen." Julian held up his hand to silence her. "I hear another boat."

How could they have missed the loud sound of the engine?

"This is the Coast Guard," boomed the voice. "Prepare to be boarded."

3

"JULIAN, it's the Coast Guard!" Dee Ann gripped his arm harder.

"So I heard," he answered, prying her fingers off him. "Their timing stinks."

"How can you say that?" she demanded, thankful her ordeal was coming to an end. "We're going to be rescued."

Julian leaned forward, his smile intimate, his arms warm. "I'm not at all sure I want to be rescued."

Dee Ann squirmed away from him. "Be serious!"

He sighed. "I was."

"Honey Bee." The voice was louder. *"Prepare to be boarded."*

"They sound angry." And Dee Ann didn't want to anger potential rescuers. "What do we do?"

"Go up on deck and meet them, I suppose." Julian stood and peered out the porthole. "Assuming they *are* the Coast Guard."

Dee Ann tried to see out, but Julian was blocking her view. "Who else would they be?"

"Pirates."

She waited for him to grin or laugh at his joke, feeble though it was. He didn't. In fact, he looked serious—serious enough to unnerve her, especially when he began to search the room.

"What are you doing?" she asked, following him around.

"Looking for something we can use to defend ourselves." He dug in the bureau drawers.

"What sort of something?" Dee Ann was reduced to following Julian and wringing her hands. It wasn't terribly effective.

"I don't know, a baseball bat. A knife." He narrowed his eyes. "A *gun.*" He held up his thumb and finger and pointed at the porthole. "Pow."

"Don't be ridiculous." The joke wasn't funny anymore. Not that it had ever been.

"I'm not kidding. There *are* pirates out here."

"Oh, really?" But there was something about his stance and the tone of his voice...no. "Are we talking buccaneers?" she scoffed. "Cannons and swords? Wooden legs and hooks?"

"Mostly guns and bad attitudes." He tried to see out the porthole from several angles, at last nodding in satisfaction. "No Jolly Roger. It's the Coast Guard." Turning back to her, he added, "I'm not altogether sure that's in our favor."

"Why ever not?" Dee Ann finger-combed her hair, trying to make herself look slightly less disreputable. She considered wrapping herself in the sheet again.

"Call it a hunch." Appearing distracted for a moment, he frowned. "Play it cool, okay? Don't make any sudden moves."

"What do you take me for? Just because I currently

resemble one of your usual empty-headed escorts doesn't mean I am one."

Julian's gaze swept over her, giving Dee Ann the sensation of being touched. The feeling rattled her. "Let's go," he said.

As he climbed the steps, Dee Ann called out, "Julian—you can't go on deck wearing just a towel!"

"Is there anything else?"

"Here." She threw the *Honey Bee* trunks at him.

He caught them in one hand, turned around, dropped his towel and stepped into them.

Dee Ann stood next to the bed, her mouth agape. He was *gorgeous*. It wasn't fair.

"Come on." He gestured for her to follow him. "I think they're on board."

"I—I..." Running to the bureau, Dee Ann latched on to the first T-shirt she found and slipped it over her head. Julian had already left. He could have waited, she grumbled to herself.

She emerged onto the deck to find a uniformed man holding a gun on Julian. When she froze, another man grabbed her arm, none too gently, and pulled her through the doorway. "No—wait! What's going on?"

Julian didn't even look at her.

"Over here, ma'am." The man gestured for Dee Ann to stand away from Julian.

She complied at once, her legs shaking.

"Sir, does this account for all personnel on board?"

"Yes." Julian's voice was very clipped and precise.

"Why are you pointing guns at us? We haven't done

anything except get lost," Dee Ann protested, alarmed by the serious expressions on the men's faces.

"Ma'am, this vessel was reported stolen."

"Stolen?"

"Be quiet, Dee Ann." Julian leveled a hard look at her.

What was wrong with him? Why didn't he tell the guardsmen what had happened? Did he enjoy being held at gunpoint?

Dee Ann certainly did not. "Officer, this boat isn't stolen. We have it."

He took out a pen and approached her. "Ma'am, are you admitting you two sailed this vessel from its berth?"

What a stupid question. How else did he think it had ended up somewhere in the Gulf of Mexico? But he looked very grave, his pen ready. Unfortunately, Dee Ann was a little—okay, a lot—fuzzy on the details of precisely how or when they'd come to be adrift on the *Honey Bee*. Julian had probably done the actual sailing, but just because Julian was the one who had maneuvered the boat didn't mean Dee Ann shouldn't own up to her role in last night's ill-considered voyage. "Well, we must have," *as any fool can see* "but I really don't remember."

"Dee Ann!" Julian said through clenched teeth.

In exasperation, she turned to him. "Julian, the sooner we untangle this mess, the sooner we can get back to shore." She addressed the Coast Guard officer. "Sir, if you'll just call or radio or however you contact people—just call Carter Belden and he'll vouch for us."

"Mr. and Mrs. Belden are the ones who reported this vessel stolen."

"Well, that was mean of them," Dee Ann stated with asperity.

A noise that sounded suspiciously like a whimper escaped Julian.

Another uniformed man approached. "No one else is on board."

"Contraband?"

"Negative."

The officer who had been talking to Dee Ann glanced at Julian, who was staring stonily ahead.

"What is your name, ma'am?"

"Dee Ann Karrenbrock." As she said it, Dee Ann wondered if she was now Dee Ann Wainright, but decided not to bring that matter up with the Coast Guard. It would only confuse things in an already confusing encounter.

"Spell it for me," he instructed as he scribbled on a clipboard. Dee Ann spelled her name.

"And yours, sir?"

Julian spoke. "I refuse to answer any questions without my attorney present."

"*Julian!*" He was being unnecessarily antagonistic. "These men are just doing their job." She turned to the officer. "He's Julian Wainright. Yes, R-I-G-H-T," she spelled out.

Julian growled.

"And he's not usually so grumpy." Dee Ann tucked a strand of hair behind her ear. "We had, uh, a late night."

"Yes, ma'am."

"Dee *Ann!*"

She darted a perplexed look at him. He wasn't behaving at all like the diplomatically urbane Julian she knew.

"Ma'am, do you have any identification?"

She smiled widely, hoping to counteract Julian's sullenness. "It's in my purse."

"Where would your purse be?"

"It's..." *uh-oh* "somewhere else." Had she thrown her purse into the ocean, as well?

The men exchanged looks. The one who had searched the *Honey Bee* shook his head.

"Do you have any other identification with you?"

Dee Ann briefly regretted shredding the marriage license. "No."

For the first time, she understood that she might have been too hasty in ignoring Julian's warnings. She glanced over at him.

He smirked.

"Sir? Identification?"

Julian didn't respond. Dee Ann wished she hadn't, either.

Sighing, the officer flipped the pages back over his clipboard. "I'm placing you both under arrest—"

"Arrest? For what?" Dee Ann asked, stunned.

"For theft of the *Honey Bee.*"

"We didn't steal this boat!" she objected. "We just borrowed it."

Julian groaned.

"Unfortunately, you forgot to tell the Beldens you

were borrowing their boat. You have the right to remain..."

Dee Ann listened with horrified fascination as she and Julian were arrested for stealing the *Honey Bee.*

This was absurd. Why didn't someone call Carter?

Or was this his revenge?

But he'd already taken his revenge, hadn't he? She thought they were friends now.

"I don't believe this," Dee Ann whispered as she and Julian were led to the deck chairs. They sat there as the Coast Guard commandeered the pilothouse.

Julian looked as though he wanted to strangle her.

She refused to accept total responsibility for their predicament. Not cooperating with the Coast Guard wouldn't have gotten them anywhere.

On the other hand, where had cooperation gotten them?

DEE ANN WAS SILENT on the way into Galveston. She wanted to ask the officers how far they'd drifted and when they could expect to arrive, but thought better of it. She could see a smudge of shoreline on the horizon, anyway.

Julian simmered. She could feel the waves of anger emanating from him.

She glanced at him several times to see if his anger had lessened. It was during one of these sidelong glances that she became aware of an optical illusion.

They were sitting on deck chairs upholstered in *Honey Bee* stripes, and with Julian attired in trunks made from the same fabric, he appeared to have vanished from the waist down, if she didn't look at his legs.

She tapped his arm, planning to point out the humor of the situation, but the cold look in his eyes stopped her. So, Dee Ann amused herself by imagining Carter wearing the trunks. He must have hated it, if she knew anything about Carter Belden.

As the afternoon wore on, Dee Ann felt better, but now she was thirsty—and hungry, too. Probably sunburned, as well.

Their captors could at least see to the creature comforts of their prisoners, she thought, making eye contact with one man. She looked away first.

Within a half hour, the *Honey Bee* was close enough to shore for Dee Ann to see that they were headed toward an unfamiliar marina.

"Excuse me, but this isn't the *Honey Bee's* slip," she said.

"It's the police compound, ma'am."

"Julian and I can direct you to the right slip, can't we, Julian?" She included him eagerly.

He rolled his eyes. "I *cannot* believe you. It must be the swimsuit. It turns its wearer into a bimbo."

"What?"

"That can be the only possible explanation for the display of obtuseness which I've seen today."

"I have no idea what you're talking about."

Julian gestured to their guard. "You see, don't you?" he asked the man.

Dee Ann saw the answering sympathy in the guard's expression and gritted her teeth. Men. If women ran the world, Dee Ann could have cleared up the misunderstanding within moments. But no. The men had to play their silly power games all the time instead of saving them for the important battles.

"Perhaps you'd care to explain why docking at the police compound is preferable to sailing into the *Honey Bee's* berth, saving the Beldens an extra trip and placing us near our cars." She was guessing—hoping—her car was still in the hotel parking lot. Anyway, she thought dryly, her suggestion was so logical, these men were sure to ignore it.

Julian's smile didn't reach his eyes. "And what good, pray tell, is being near our cars?"

He'd lost it completely, Dee Ann decided. She'd have to be the strong one. "So we can go home," she explained gently, as though to a child.

"Dee Ann," he said, his tone matching hers, "we're under arrest."

"But that's a mistake. Whatever happened to *innocent until proven guilty?*" she said, raising her voice.

The guard cleared his throat. "Ma'am, you confessed."

"I did no such thing!"

"Think, darling." Julian patted her head. "You remember how, don't you?"

Dee Ann glared at him, but as she glared, she thought back over the conversation she'd had with the guardsman. "I suppose some of what I said could have been misinterpreted," she admitted stiffly, inching away from Julian.

They were preparing to dock. For the first time, he

looked nervous. Straining to see the man in the pilothouse, Julian asked their guard, "Does he know how to handle a boat this size?"

The guard shrugged.

"Tell him to take it easy, okay?" he told the guard. Turning back to Dee Ann, he muttered, "Nikki will kill us if anything happens to her boat."

"You're more concerned about this boat than you are about me."

"No, I'm more afraid of Nikki than I am of you."

"I'll have to ask her for tips."

Their guard was joined by another man. "Stand up with your arms extended in front of you."

"Why?" Dee Ann asked.

"Just do it, darling," Julian taunted.

She was going to get him for that. Dee Ann stood and held out her arms. "What now? Are ya' gonna cuff me?" she mouthed off.

"Yes, ma'am," the officer replied as he handcuffed her.

She saw it. She felt it. But she didn't believe it.

Julian was cuffed, as well.

This had to be a nightmare. That's it. She was still asleep.

But she pulled at her hands and felt the metal. She'd never even seen a pair of handcuffs up close before.

And never thought she would, either.

"This way, folks."

Barefoot, Dee Ann and Julian were led to a waiting police car.

"I've never been so humiliated in my life," she declared as they were handed into the custody of Galveston police officers.

"Never?" Julian asked. "Not even when you marched down the aisle and your groom wasn't there?"

"He would have been there if it hadn't been for you."

"True."

Nevertheless, that had been humiliating, as well. But even being jilted didn't compare with being handcuffed and half-naked in a police car. "I can't help noticing that you've played a feature role in the most awful moments of my life, Julian."

He started to say something, probably something nasty, then caught himself. "I'm so sorry, Dee Ann. I truly am." The last was a whisper.

She was always a sucker for remorse. Sighing, she said, "At least we won't run into anybody we know. And once Carter straightens everything out, we can go home and forget this ever happened."

He managed a jaunty grin. "Someday we'll laugh about this."

Dee Ann shook her head. "I don't think so."

"No." He sighed. "No, you're right."

Staring out the window, Dee Ann saw her reflection in the side mirror and wished she hadn't.

Her hair looked like blond spaghetti and mascara ringed her eyes. The words on her T-shirt were backward. Looking down at herself, she shifted until she could read the entire slogan: *I Don't Do Mornings.*

Dee Ann didn't know whether to laugh or cry. The emotions warred, then seemed to cancel each other out.

And Julian still managed to look human. More than

human. Carter was stockier than Julian, so the trunks rode low on his hips, exposing a taut abdomen maintained with a precise number of stomach crunches daily, she guessed. His beard actually increased his attractiveness, but in a different, more untamed way.

Dee Ann looked untamed, but in a different, more slovenly way. *When I get through this, and I will, I am going to treat myself to a day at a spa. I'll get the works.*

Visualizing a day of herbal wraps and facials helped Dee Ann endure the ride in the police car. Exposed by the T-shirt, her thighs were in contact with the vinyl seat, the same seat upon which actual felons had sat. Her flesh crawled and she shivered.

"You holding up okay?" Julian mouthed.

And what would he do about it if she weren't? But Dee Ann appreciated his show of concern, so she nodded and found that maintaining a composed front for Julian actually helped.

She'd even convinced herself that her situation wasn't so bad.

Then they had to walk into the station.

People gawked at them. Didn't they have anything better to do than spend a Sunday afternoon outside the police station?

Or...or perhaps they were decent, concerned parents showing their children that people who flouted the law were hauled off to jail. She, Dee Ann Karrenbrock, was being used as an example to frighten children into behaving well.

She emerged from the police car, trying to look innocent and misunderstood.

"Stay close," Julian whispered.

Dee Ann opened her mouth to ask why, then thought better of it. Perhaps if she'd paid attention to Julian before, they wouldn't be on their way to jail.

"Ouch!" She stumbled forward as she stepped on a sharp piece of shell gravel.

"Keep moving!" a policeman barked.

"Can't you see she's hurt her foot?" Julian snapped, and bent down.

He was jerked upright.

"I said, keep moving!" The officer accompanied this with a shove, not hard enough to send Julian sprawling, but forceful enough to show he meant business.

"Sorry," Julian said. "I'm afraid I'm not up on prisoner etiquette."

"I'm okay, Julian," Dee Ann told him. He'd exposed himself to rough treatment on her behalf, which gave him some much-needed points in the plus column.

"Ma'am, we'll have someone take a look at that foot when we get inside," the officer informed her.

Limping more than necessary to make the man feel ashamed, Dee Ann negotiated her way into the police station. Once she stepped onto the tile floor, it was apparent that her foot was bleeding slightly.

The cut wasn't deep, and once it was bandaged, Julian and Dee Ann were led into a room and handcuffed to a bench.

The fluorescent lights turned everything a sickly green. Even Julian looked haggard, which meant Dee Ann must look like death warmed over. No wonder the police thought they were criminals. They *looked* like criminals. But anybody without stage makeup on would look like a criminal in this place, Dee Ann thought.

"I'm calling Saunders as soon as they let us," Julian said.

"Why don't you call Carter so he can come and tell these overly efficient officers that we aren't thieves?"

"Because Saunders is a lawyer and Carter isn't."

"We don't need a lawyer! We need the owners of the boat to explain that everything is okay!" Dee Ann couldn't believe Julian was going to waste his phone call on the Belden Industries company lawyer. "I think the fewer people who know about this, the better, don't you?"

"You mean, other than the Coast Guard and the Galveston police?" He pursed his mouth. "'That's Karrenbrock with two Rs,'" he mimicked in a falsetto.

Dee Ann looked away.

Julian sighed. "If you want to use your one phone call trying to reach Carter, be my guest. But I strongly advise you to call your own lawyer."

"I don't want to call *anybody!* I just want this entire mess to go away!" She covered her face with the hand that wasn't handcuffed to the bench. "I look awful and I feel even worse. I'm hungry and thirsty—don't they ever feed prisoners?"

"We haven't been processed yet—"

"Processed!" She stared at him. "You mean, fingerprinted? You mean, having my picture taken holding one of those numbers?" Her voice rose.

"Calm down. Saunders will get us out of here," Julian promised as a policeman approached them.

"You can each make your phone call," he informed them.

"Could you bring us some water?" Julian asked before he was freed from the bench. "We've had nothing for hours."

"Sure."

The policeman didn't seem at all put out by Julian's request and Dee Ann relaxed a little. Perhaps they hadn't been given water because they hadn't asked for it. The police couldn't read minds.

"Dee Ann, I'm going to call Saunders. You call your lawyer or your parents and have *them* call your lawyer."

"*No!*" Shocked, she stared at him. "Julian, I can't call my parents! What would they think?" She clutched his arm. "They mustn't know about this. No one must find out about this. Make Saunders promise."

"What do you think he'll do, send out press releases?"

Dee Ann chose her next words very carefully. "I realize Saunders is a personal friend, however, under these circumstances, perhaps someone more...forceful might be appropriate."

Julian gave her a wry smile. "You've gone from 'we don't need a lawyer' to wanting a barracuda?"

At that moment, they were each handed a paper cup of water. Dee Ann drained hers greedily.

"More?" the policeman asked and Dee Ann nodded.

"Don't underestimate Saunders," Julian advised her while they waited. "He acts like a wimp except when he's practicing law. In a fix like this, there's no one else I'd rather have in my corner."

4

"PICK UP, Saunders," Julian called into the phone when he got the lawyer's answering machine. "Pick up!"

Nothing. A queasy feeling entirely unrelated to his hangover settled in Julian's stomach. What if Saunders wasn't at home?

The man had to be there. He couldn't be out with friends—Nikki, Carter and Julian *were* his only friends. Nikki and Carter were newly married and even the socially obtuse Saunders wouldn't tag along with them today.

Julian refused to hang up. "Saunders! It's Julian. Wake up, man! I know you're there... *Saunders, you coward, pick up!* This isn't funny...don't think I haven't remembered where that wedding license came from."

During the long ride into port, Julian had concentrated on piecing together the elusive fragments he remembered from yesterday evening. It was all coming back to him, or enough to guess the rest, anyway.

Saunders hadn't worn his tuxedo since he was to be the best man at Dee Ann and Carter's wedding-that-wasn't. He'd thought it a real riot to find the old wedding license in his breast pocket as he stood up for Carter at his remarriage to Nikki.

Maybe he wasn't at home, after all. "Saunders," Julian said crisply, "I need you pronto. Dee Ann and I are at the Galveston police station. We've been arrested—"

"Dang blast it, Julian, why didn't you say so," Saunders broke in.

"Why didn't you pick up the phone!" Relief made Julian snap.

"Didn't want to be yelled at," Saunders whimpered. "I've got the mother of all headaches."

Julian's gaze roamed the interior of the police station, settled on the bedraggled blonde—possibly his wife—and he sighed, "No, Saunders, I believe I have that honor."

"Two minutes," an officer signaled Julian.

He nodded and spoke to Saunders. "Listen, get hold of Carter and tell him what happened—"

"What *did* happen?"

Julian sighed and leaned his head against the cool gray-green wall. "Dee Ann and I apparently went for a sail on the *Honey Bee* and fell asleep."

"Yeah, right." Saunders snickered.

"It's not funny. The Coast Guard found us after Nikki and Carter reported the boat stolen."

"Too bad. It looked like you and Dee Ann—"

"Find Carter and get down here!"

Silence.

"Saunders?"

"They're on their honeymoon, Julian."

"How can they be on their honeymoon when we had their boat? No, don't explain. I don't care where they are. I just want you to get us out of here!"

"I'll do my best," Saunders said, but he sounded doubtful.

It wasn't a good sign.

Julian hitched up his borrowed swim trunks and was led into the processing area.

Dee Ann was already sitting on an armless chair in front of a desk, her legs together, her hands folded primly in her lap. She was doing her best to stay controlled, Julian knew, but he also knew how close she was to breaking down.

After that conversation with Saunders, *he* was close to doing the same.

The amazing thing was how sexy Dee Ann managed to look with her hair windblown and her eye makeup smudged. Julian was surprised that he found her untamed look appealing. It had been her carefully controlled appearance that had attracted him to her in the first place. She always wore her blond hair in a twist or a chignon, showing off her long neck and high cheekbones.

Julian was a neck connoisseur and Dee Ann had a glorious one, just made for nibbling.

He liked the regal way she held herself, too. Unfortunately, that regal air wasn't so attractive when he found himself on the opposite side of a takeover war.

Her father was supposedly the business shark in the family, but Dee Ann had been the one to watch, Julian had discovered. Having once underestimated her, he'd vowed not to do so again.

So he found himself embroiled in an odd relationship with Dee Ann Karrenbrock—he admired her business acumen, but they were corporate enemies. He was attracted to her, but he didn't necessarily like her.

She'd treated him badly—but he would have treated her the same way, he admitted to himself with a shrug. He was just incensed because she'd dumped him first.

For Carter. She'd chosen Carter over him. That had hurt Julian's pride. If it had been anybody else...

But Carter had offered her marriage and marriage wasn't on Julian's agenda.

Or it hadn't been until Saunders found that blasted wedding license and Dee Ann had looked so... interesting last night. Julian had begun to see possibilities. She was softer and more vulnerable. The ocean breezes had loosened tendrils of her hair and she'd taken off her shoes.

It had taken guts to come to Carter's wedding and he'd admired her for that. But admiration wasn't a solid enough foundation for a relationship. However, lust was a perfectly valid temporary foundation on which he'd obviously built last night.

Temporary being the operative word, he reminded himself. Dee Ann was appealingly vulnerable right now, but Dee Ann was not often vulnerable.

"Hey," he said as he sat in the chair next to her. "Just a little longer. Saunders is on his way down."

"WHERE IN THE *HELL* is Saunders?" Julian paced in the holding cell and tried to peer down the hallway.

"Don't know, man," said Julian's fellow inmate, a large, docile-looking man.

Fortunately, all the Saturday-night drunks had been

cleared out and only this other man remained with Julian. He hoped Dee Ann was faring as well.

Gripping the bars in frustration, he shook them ineffectually. "This whole thing is a complete misunderstanding."

"Yeah, man. You just keep telling yourself that."

"It's *true.*" Julian ran his fingers through his hair. Was it his imagination, or had his hairline receded a few millimeters since his incarceration? "This is a ridiculous waste of taxpayers' money. I shouldn't be in jail, I haven't done anything wrong."

"Boy, I hear that." The other man shook his head in agreement.

Julian couldn't believe he was actually in a jail cell. Why couldn't he and Dee Ann have stayed on the benches? "I'm a responsible citizen and I resent being treated like a criminal!"

"Right on, brother."

With such an appreciative audience, Julian warmed to his theme. "I don't have so much as an outstanding parking ticket. You'd think that would count for something, but no." He raised his voice so the guards could hear.

"Don't I know it." The man stretched out on the concrete platform that served as both bed and bench.

Julian envied him his calm. How could the man stand it in here? The entire situation was intolerable. "I ask you, what good does it do to lead a responsible life?"

"None at all," his companion agreed mournfully. "They're gonna getcha no matter whatcha do."

A guard was approaching. "If they're going to treat me like a criminal, I might as well *be one!*"

Julian's cell mate raised his hands. "Hallelujah!"

Julian felt much better, and even more so when he saw who his guard was leading to the cell.

"Saunders!"

The lawyer whistled. "Nice outfit."

Julian refrained from punching him through the bars.

"Ya ready to be sprung?" Saunders said in a bad gangster accent.

"Where have you been?" Julian demanded as the guard unlocked the cell.

"Trying to find Carter and Nikki." Saunders exhaled. "And I did—finally."

"Great." Julian walked out of the cell a free man, or closer to being free than he'd been for the past few hours.

As the guard closed and locked the cell, Julian called to his former cell mate, "Keep the faith."

The man responded with a thumbs-up.

"Friend of yours?" Saunders asked.

"Just another misunderstood citizen."

"Yeah, but he was misunderstood with a houseful of stolen electronics and jewelry," said the guard. "Probably not worth as much as the yacht, though."

Saunders laughed until he was silenced by Julian's glare.

Dee Ann, and Carter and Nikki Belden were waiting for them by the front desk.

Even in the sickly surroundings of the police station, the newly married Nikki was radiant, her freckled face animated as she spoke to a policeman. Carter had linked his hand through his wife's and looked content.

The usually elegant Dee Ann did not compare well. The poor woman looked as though she were shell-shocked. Even though she'd brought a lot of this on herself, Julian felt an unwilling sympathy. As far as he knew, before now, none of his dates had ever had reason to regret an evening with him.

Now, after this ghastly experience, he at least was surrounded by friends. She had no one. No one except him.

He ignored the fact that she was alone by choice as a surge of protectiveness prompted him to make his way to stand next to her. "Are you all right?"

She nodded stiffly.

Nikki caught sight of him. "Julian! You're wearing Carter's *Honey Bee* trunks."

Behind her, Carter struggled not to laugh.

Dee Ann tugged at the hem of her T-shirt and refused to meet anyone's eyes.

"You know how it is, Nikki. When in Rome..." Julian shrugged, but felt like a fool. Couldn't Dee Ann have found *anything* else for them to wear?

"Officer?" Saunders said. "May I see those papers?" The lawyer went off, presumably to take care of all the legalities.

"We're so sorry," Nikki said. "I didn't realize you and Dee Ann were aboard the *Honey Bee* when I called the police."

Julian held up a hand. "I should be apologizing to you. Both of you," he said, including Carter. "I don't think we *intended* to take the *Honey Bee*. Certainly not on a prolonged cruise in the Gulf of Mexico."

"You can tell us all about it on the way home." Carter met Julian's eyes over the top of Nikki's head. *Were you insane?* his look asked.

Julian glanced at Dee Ann. She stared stoically ahead, her arms wrapped around herself.

Now that he thought about it, insanity was as good an explanation as any.

"All's well that ends well," warbled Saunders, waving the papers. "We're free to go."

"Nikki and I will drive you and Dee Ann home," Carter stated and Julian accepted gratefully. He didn't know where his car keys were, anyway.

"I'll be right behind you, Julian." Saunders rubbed his hands together. "Boy, I can't *wait*—"

"Saunders!" Nikki jerked her head toward Dee Ann, who was standing apart from them.

She was doing a credible job of appearing unconcerned about her appearance, but Julian caught her tugging again at the hem of Nikki's T-shirt.

He wondered if Nikki knew what Dee Ann was wearing underneath it.

"Will you be able to get into your house?" he asked her as they all walked toward the exit.

Her eyes widened and Julian saw the panic when she remembered that she didn't have her purse. "Don't worry," he reassured her. "You can come home with me. Saunders has a key to my penthouse. We'll find a locksmith for your place."

Her eyes flashed. She wanted to tell him off, he knew,

but at the moment she wasn't in a position to. She needed him and she knew it.

And Julian discovered he liked being needed. What an odd feeling.

"Holy cow!" Saunders stopped at the front door to the police station. "Look at all the people out there. What's going on?"

Nikki stood on tiptoe and peered out the tiny rectangular window. "Reporters." She glanced at Carter. "And photographers."

Everyone stared at Saunders.

"*I* didn't tell anyone!" he protested. "And I object to the fact that you all immediately suspected that—"

"Quiet, Saunders." Julian pressed his lips together tightly. "I know who tipped them off." He shot a sizzling look toward Dee Ann.

Color seeped into her cheeks. "Surely you aren't implying that *I*—"

"'I'm Dee Ann Karrenbrock and this is Julian Wainright,'" he mimicked. "Haven't you ever heard of police scanners? Don't you know the press monitors them?" he railed. "A nice slow Sunday afternoon...and 'Karrenbrock with two Rs' comes over the scanner."

"Karrenbrock has three Rs," Saunders corrected.

"Shut *up,* Saunders!" ordered three voices in unison.

"Not possessing your apparently *vast* experience with the police, I was attempting to cooperate," Dee Ann was at last goaded into defending herself.

"Oh, and they appreciated that, let me tell you." Julian ran his fingers through his hair again. He *was* losing hair. Dee Ann was making him go prematurely bald.

Yes, but you shouldn't have taken out your frustration on her. He started to apologize, and stopped. She was mad, but she looked a lot stronger now. Anything was better than that whipped-dog look she'd had earlier. Julian decided to leave well enough alone.

"I think we can make a run for it out back," Carter said. "We won't avoid all the press, but the longer we wait around, the more reporters will arrive."

"Let's all walk in a group and look happy and casual," Nikki said, glancing at a tight-lipped Dee Ann. "The press hates happy and casual. It isn't newsworthy."

"Well, that's us, isn't it?" Julian draped his arms around both Dee Ann and Nikki. "Smile, Dee Ann," he said with a fake one of his own. "You don't look happy. I will say, though, that you've nailed down the 'casual' part."

Dee Ann pushed his arm away and marched through the police station.

"You know, Julian," Carter said, "I've been meaning to compliment you on those swim trunks. They look much better on you than they ever did on me. I think you should have them." He clapped Julian on the shoulder.

"*Carter!*" An outraged Nikki poked him in the ribs. "You'll break up the set."

Saunders was already peering out the back door. "Pipe down, children. If we're going to make a break for it, now's the time." He checked to see that they were all behind him, then pushed open the door.

"I can't." Dee Ann froze.

"What do you mean, you *can't?* You want to spend the night in jail?" Julian asked in exasperation.

She shook her head. "Tell the police to send the reporters away."

"As far as I am aware, they aren't breaking any laws," Saunders said. "They have a right to report the news. And, unfortunately, the daughter of Victor Karrenbrock is news. Stealing a forty-foot yacht is news. Stealing it from a honeymooning couple, one of whom you, yourself, were planning to marry is news. Add to that the takeover attempt—"

"Saunders." Julian gave his friend a quelling look then turned to Dee Ann. "Take my hand." He held it out to her.

She backed away.

"Take my hand."

Their gazes met and Julian saw the wildness leave her eyes. She slipped her hand into his. He squeezed it reassuringly and nodded to Saunders.

Saunders held the door and they trooped out into the evening sunshine as if they were leaving a museum instead of a police station.

The lucky reporters who'd camped out back spotted them immediately and surged forward.

Julian and the others forgot casual and happy at the first shouts. Cameras clicked and microphones were thrust in front of them as they ran the press gauntlet. A camera crew from the local television station had just arrived. Julian could hear Saunders repeating "No comment" over and over.

Dee Ann clung to his hand so hard he thought her

grip would cut off his circulation. She ducked her head and tried to hide her face by pulling up her T-shirt, thus looking very guilty.

By the time they reached Carter's car, Julian knew there had been enough photographs and taped footage to plaster them all over the evening news and tomorrow's papers.

"We shouldn't have run from them," he said as Carter tried to negotiate his car through the parking lot without hitting anyone. "We should have given them a statement. Now they'll just print speculation." Or pictures of Dee Ann's legs.

With the help of the police, Carter managed to get a head start out of the parking lot. "Are they following?"

"Not yet," Julian said, watching out the back window. "But they will."

"Carter, you're going too fast," Nikki warned.

"I don't have much choice," he said, slowing down.

"Better turn off this street. I think we're being followed," Julian instructed. "Or is that Saunders?"

"Don't worry about Saunders," Nikki said. "We need to get Dee Ann and Julian out of sight."

"Please take me directly home," Dee Ann said in a quiet voice. "My parents should be there. They'll let me inside."

"Are you sure?" Julian asked. He retrieved Carter's cellular phone from the front seat and offered it to her. "There's no way they won't ask questions when they see you."

Dee Ann accepted the phone. "Better to explain now than let them hear about it on the ten o'clock news," she said evenly. Once they'd left the police station, Dee Ann seemed to have recovered her poise.

Julian wished they were alone. His usual stock of glib parting lines was useless and he was going to have to ad-lib. He didn't want an audience.

What on earth was appropriate to say under the circumstances?

Dee Ann probably never wanted to see him again.

But did he want to see her?

JUST A FEW MORE BLOCKS and Dee Ann would never have to face any of these people again. She could hold herself together for five more minutes and then she was going to fall apart.

No one had answered at home, but Dee Ann didn't care. She'd break a window before she'd spend one more moment with them. Of course, breaking a window would set off the burglar alarm. And the police would come and, with her luck, probably arrest her again.

At least now she knew the routine. Hysterical laughter bubbled inside of her.

The Karrenbrock house was a lovely Victorian home in the heart of old Galveston, a very staid neighborhood with other equally lovely homes lining the boulevard.

Carter turned onto the street and Dee Ann relaxed a bit. A few seconds more and she'd escape from this car and her companions and this hideous situation.

Julian would probably try to be noble and escort her to the door. Dee Ann didn't want a half-naked man being noble on her porch, so she gripped the door handle, planning to leap out then send them on their way.

"Stop!" Nikki pointed to a van with a satellite dish on top. "That's a news van."

Carter slammed on the brakes and three people uttered the same four-letter word in unison. Dee Ann had been thinking of another four-letter word, but was willing to go along with the majority.

"They're staking out your house, Dee Ann," Carter said, "but I don't think they've spotted us yet."

"It's only a matter of time," Nikki murmured.

Dee Ann bit her lip. What now?

She looked at Julian.

Julian looked at Dee Ann's frozen face. "Drive to our building," he ordered.

"We'll have to pass the van in order to turn around," Nikki said.

"And you know they'll recognize this car." Julian met Carter's eyes in the rearview mirror.

Carter grinned.

Julian liked those grins. "Hang on," he said to Dee Ann.

"Carter..." Nikki generally *didn't* like those grins, he knew.

Carter had already pulled into a driveway. Backing up, he turned the car around and roared the wrong way down the boulevard, a maniacal grin still in place.

They nearly collided head-on with Saunders.

"Did you see his eyes bug out?" Carter whooped.

"Well, he's turning around," Julian reported, as he

saw Saunders make an impressive recovery. "And the news van is in hot pursuit."

"Be careful, Carter," Nikki warned.

In their first break of the day, they weren't arrested for speeding as they drove to the apartment building.

But that was the only break.

"I hate cellular phones," Julian said when he spied one of the satellite vans parked in front of his apartment building. A woman with a microphone was arguing with the doorman. "Everybody's got one and there isn't an advantage anymore."

Carter whipped into a parking lot down the street. "Shall we try the office?"

"Yeah," Julian said. "But call security, first."

They beat the news media and security was waiting for them. Abandoning the car, they ran inside, Nikki, Carter and Julian laughing and filled with the rush that comes from besting one's opponent in a hard-fought fight.

The last time they'd felt this way was when they'd regained control of Belden Industries from Karrenbrock Ventures. From Dee Ann.

Dee Ann. Julian sobered immediately.

Dee Ann had gone to the reception desk and was using the telephone. Her eyes squeezed shut and she very carefully replaced the receiver.

The whipped-dog look was back in place, he saw. What was he going to have to do, pick another argument with her? He didn't want to argue anymore and he bet Dee Ann didn't, either.

Carter and Nikki were standing at the elevators, obviously about to go up to Carter's office.

Julian gestured to Dee Ann. "Come on, we can hole up in Carter's office for a while."

"Forever?" Dee Ann asked with a tired smile as they entered the elevator.

Julian knew how she felt. "Long enough to clean up and eat."

Dee Ann sighed and closed her eyes again.

He was beginning to feel the effects of the day, himself, and he gripped the brass railing as the elevator sped upward.

Carter and Nikki were suspiciously silent and Julian caught them exchanging looks. Great. He owed them an explanation and probably a lot more than that.

What a mess he'd made of everything.

The elevator opened on the top floor and Julian stepped onto the plush carpeting. He'd never fully appreciated the carpeting, but then, he'd never walked barefoot on it before.

"Dee Ann, you can use the shower in my office," Carter offered, unlocking the door to a corner suite.

"I don't think I've ever seen this part of your office, Carter," she said.

"All the conveniences of home."

"I'll try to find you something to wear," Nikki said, disappearing into another room. "For now, use the robe on the hook."

Dee Ann nodded wearily and closed the bathroom door.

Julian swayed. "Food. We haven't eaten since your reception."

Carter eyed him a moment. "What were you thinking, Julian?" he asked as he walked over to the kitchenette.

Julian knew he wasn't referring to food. "It's a long story."

"Summarize."

"I got drunk."

After shooting Julian an incredulous look, Carter opened the small refrigerator and pawed through the shelves. "In all the years I've known you—all the ups and downs—I have never known you to become drunk."

"I did last night." He explained about Bob's wine as Carter unearthed packages of crackers, soup and caviar.

"This is the best I can do." Carter filled two coffee mugs with tap water and handed Julian a packet of dried soup.

"Things are looking up." Normally, Julian would suggest a nice crisp white wine to accompany the snack, but he wanted a clear head.

"And was my former fiancée drowning her sorrows?"

"Hardly," Julian retorted and shoved a mug with the soup mixture into the microwave. "She had a little problem with roses and antihistamines."

"You could have lied." Carter mixed a second mug.

"Your ego will survive. Any cheese?"

Carter shook his head. "We weren't planning to come

back here for several weeks," he reminded Julian with a sidelong glance.

The microwave dinged. "Let me take this to Dee Ann and I'll tell you all about our doomed voyage." Julian needed time to pick and choose exactly what information to pass on to Carter.

Though Carter was his friend, Julian wasn't about to reveal everything that had happened.

He could hear the shower running and rapped loudly on the door. "Dee Ann?"

The shower stopped.

"I'm setting some soup and crackers next to the door."

"Thanks," he heard before the shower started again.

What discipline. Julian stole a cracker. As hungry as he was, he would have broken down the door to get to the food.

Saunders burst into the room at the exact moment the microwave finished heating Julian's soup. "Well, thanks for waiting."

"Did you outrun the reporters?" Julian drank his soup too quickly.

"No." Saunders reached for the crackers and Julian snatched them away. "I *would* have if security hadn't locked the doors."

"Oops," Carter said.

"What did you tell them?" Julian asked, munching on a cracker. He just might live, he thought.

"I made up a story, and since no one has bothered to consult with me, you all are going to have to agree to it." Saunders was looking very self-important.

"And that story is...?" Julian opened the caviar.

"I told them that you and Ms. Karrenbrock had gone aboard the *Honey Bee* to make certain arrangements for the bride and groom, and in moving the boat, you had engine trouble and drifted into the gulf, where you were rescued this afternoon by the Coast Guard. Unfortunately, the Beldens had reported the *Honey Bee* stolen, and the authorities were only acting on that information. Et cetera, et cetera."

"I'm impressed, Saunders. That's a great story." Julian lifted his mug in a toast.

Carter grunted. "Makes us look like fools for overreacting."

Julian grinned. "That's why it's such a great story."

5

DEE ANN FELT almost human again. It's a shame she didn't look as good. Her nose glowed a bright pink between eyes ringed with the remnants of a very stubborn waterproof mascara. Carter, naturally, didn't stock cold cream in his private washroom.

Neither did he stock her regular shampoo and conditioner. Her hair felt like wet straw. Attempting to finger-comb it met with limited success, so Dee Ann gave up and wrapped a towel around her head, hoping for a spa-chic effect.

She was going to have to face them all sometime. It might as well be now. Tightening the belt on Carter's terry-cloth robe, she drew a deep breath and opened the door of the small executive bathroom.

The office was empty.

A reprieve. She grabbed the soup and crackers Julian had left beside the door and retreated.

She was famished. Sitting on the toilet lid, she gulped the lukewarm soup, thinking it was the best dried chicken-noodle soup mix she'd ever tasted.

The soup soothed her rolling stomach. Sighing, Dee Ann balanced the mug on the edge of the sink. Time to ponder her future.

As attractive as the proposition was, she couldn't

hide out in Carter's bathroom forever. At some point, she'd have to face her parents, her friends—and the Galveston business community. But did it have to be right away?

Dee Ann munched on a cracker. She'd managed to make herself the talk of the town all summer long. First, her short engagement to the owner of Karrenbrock Ventures' biggest rival, then all of Galveston had witnessed her being jilted, made worse by the appendicitis story Julian and his cohorts had spread about as Carter's excuse. Then her takeover attempt failed, then Carter announced his engagement to his ex-wife and now this.

Why oh why had she allowed Nikki to talk her into attending the wedding? She'd known it was a bad idea. Her mother had known it too, and had said so at length.

Speaking of her mother, Felicia Karrenbrock was going to have a fit when she learned about this latest mess. Dee Ann whimpered. She couldn't endure another second of her mother's endless moaning and carrying-on.

Wait until her family saw the news. Fortunately, or unfortunately, depending on how one looked at it, her parents didn't seem to be at home this evening. Maybe they'd miss the news on television.

But they wouldn't miss the morning paper.

Dee Ann didn't want to see either the news or the paper.

And she certainly didn't want to be there when her parents did. She knew that as soon as the first report aired, there would be phone calls from "concerned" acquaintances eager for details. There would be horrified looks directed at Dee Ann. There would be shrieking when Dee Ann confirmed the reports. There would be wailing and how-could-yous. And then there would be crying. Lots of crying.

Dee Ann finished the last of the crackers and studied the brown and forest green wallpaper. Carter's bathroom wasn't such a bad place to hide out, she thought. She could live with this color scheme.

Maybe if she was really quiet, they'd forget about her and she could sneak out and raid the kitchenette. Look at all the nutrients they packed into soup mix these days. Why, one could live on soup. There might even be a beef-flavored variety. And the Beldens wouldn't need it. Weren't they going on a honeymoon?

There was a knock on the door. Drat. There went her plans.

"Dee Ann?" Julian's voice.

"Nobody here by that name," she called, hoping he'd go away.

He laughed. "I found something for you to wear."

"Oh? Something better than Carter's bathrobe?"

"Something more expensive than Carter's bathrobe."

That sounded promising. Dee Ann opened the door and Julian handed her a paisley bundle. "What's this?"

"Silk pajamas."

"Whose?"

Julian smiled, his gaze roving over her. "Mine."

She threw them at him and slammed the door. Had he no shame? Offering her his *pajamas* for her to parade around in as if they were lovers.

But weren't they lovers? Dee Ann wished she could remember.

"Come on, Dee Ann. I'll let you wear the top *and* the bottoms."

"How can you be so..." Words failed her.

"Practical?" Julian supplied. "Look, I keep a set in my office for when I sleep here."

"What kind of man keeps a set of silk pajamas at the office?"

"A practical man," he replied. "I wouldn't want to sleep in my clothes and I don't think it's appropriate to sleep au naturel at the office. Ergo, I keep a set of tasteful, opaque sleepwear on hand."

Only Julian.

"Think of them as a lounging outfit. Very fashionable this season. I swear, you could put a belt around the shirt and wear them out on the street. Nobody would ever know."

"Is that what you're leading up to?"

She heard an angry sigh. "I'm not leading up to anything except the shower in my office. I'm going to leave the pajamas outside the door. Wear them or not. It's a matter of supreme indifference to me."

By pressing her ear to the door, Dee Ann could hear the soft footfalls as Julian padded away.

Showering in *his* office? He and Carter had all the comforts of home. In fact, why did they bother to rent apartments?

Dee Ann cracked open the door and slithered the pajamas inside.

Actually, Julian and Carter *were* being practical. How

many times had she hurried home to change before a banquet or business dinner and arrived rushed and out of breath?

As she slipped on Julian's pajamas, Dee Ann was already redesigning her office. It was obvious that she'd have to come out of her self-imposed retirement, since she doubted she'd have a husband and family any time soon.

And, she brightened, she could *live* at her office. That's it, she'd bury herself in work and never have to face anyone again.

She'd call her interior decorator at once.

Now all Dee Ann had to do was figure out where she could hole up until the work was done.

JULIAN FELT almost human again now that the stench of jail was washed off. Wrapping himself in a white terry robe exactly like the one Dee Ann was wearing brought her to mind.

Dee Ann. He shook his head. Apparently, he'd acquired a stray. A hostile stray. Now what was he to do?

Offer her a decent meal, for one thing. Julian walked across the Oriental carpet to his desk and flipped through his Rolodex.

Which of his usual restaurants would deliver a meal on a Sunday evening? Or should he call out for pizza?

No, no. He wanted meat. A lot of meat. Prime rib, rare. With a stout burgundy.

Dee Ann probably wanted grilled chicken breast with rice pilaf. Or a salad.

She was going to get prime rib, rare. With a stout burgundy.

And something chocolate. Women liked chocolate. Julian had never met one yet who declined a piece of Margaux's chocolate-raspberry-truffle cheesecake.

He placed the order.

Saunders came in just as Julian was hanging up the telephone. "Hotel security found your cars. They'll keep an eye on them tonight."

"Good. I hope Dee Ann keeps a spare set of keys." Julian opened the coat closet where he kept a change of clothing. Except dress shoes, he noted. There was nothing to wear but a pair of running shoes.

"Carter is raiding petty cash for you, but Nikki isn't having any luck with clothes for Dee Ann. They don't wear the same size."

"I know." Julian stopped in the act of scribbling a reminder to himself about outfitting the closet with a spare set of shoes. A vision of Dee Ann in the *Honey Bee* swimsuit formed in his mind. He smiled, then sighed. "I lent her my pajamas."

"The silk ones Nikki gave you?" Saunders asked, his eyebrows raised.

Julian dragged a white shirt off a hanger. "Yep."

"Interesting choice." Saunders sat on the corner of Julian's desk and swung his leg back and forth. "You said there was something you wanted my opinion on?"

Yes, there was, but Julian didn't quite know how to begin. "Client-lawyer confidentiality?"

"Damn." Saunders stuck out his lower lip. "I was hoping I wouldn't have to wear my lawyer hat."

"If you don't feel comfortable, I can always go—"

"Yes, yes, go ahead." Saunders waved his hands.

Julian told him what he remembered about the wedding license. When Saunders didn't act surprised, Julian felt ill. "So, who signed the thing, anyway? Did you?"

"No. Roy Peabody did."

Their rabble-rousing lawyer friend. Julian exhaled in relief and finished buttoning his shirt. "I should have known. Even in school, Roy was always pulling stunts like that. But *you*—" he jabbed a finger at Saunders "—it was rotten of you to wave around Carter's old license. Think how Dee Ann felt."

"Excuse me, but both you and Dee Ann thought it was a wonderful idea. Fate, you called it."

"*I* called it fate?" Julian had a shadowy memory of walking along the beach with a Dee Ann who was skipping. Dee Ann wasn't the skipping type, or at least he hadn't thought so. He remembered feeling happy—okay, that was probably Bob's wine—and wondering why he'd put off marriage so long. It seemed silly. As he and Dee Ann walked barefoot in the sand, he'd thought about the sort of woman he'd be willing to spend the rest of his life with. Somewhere out on the Galveston beach, this vision of the perfect wife took on Dee Ann's appearance.

They'd returned to the reception and separated for a while as the bride and groom were toasted. "I remember talking to you about Dee Ann," Julian said to Saunders. "*That's* when you showed me the wedding license you still had in your pocket. I remember now."

Nodding, Saunders wrinkled his forehead. "And you said how convenient."

Convenient? It had been anything but. Julian stepped into his pants. "Dee Ann and I couldn't read the signature and for a while I was afraid the minister might have played a doubleheader."

"Nope. It was Roy."

"So there's no way anything legally binding happened. That's a relief." Julian had zipped his pants and buckled his belt, before it registered that Saunders hadn't said anything.

Saunders had stopped swinging his leg. When Julian looked at him inquiringly, he asked, "Is there a possibility that you'd *want* it to be legal?"

"No...why?" Julian rolled his eyes. "You don't think I'm in love with Dee Ann Karrenbrock, do you?"

Saunders cleared his throat. "I wasn't referring to your emotional state, but to the possibility of issue."

Julian was bent over tying his running shoes. They looked horrible with his dress slacks. "What do you mean, issue?"

"A child," Saunders said bluntly.

Julian's heart stopped, then resumed pounding with such force that he thought his head would explode. He sat up too quickly and felt dizzy.

Darkness ringed his vision and he could hear Saunders as though from a great distance.

"Julian? It...isn't a possibility, is it? I just mentioned it to cover all the bases—Julian? *Julian*. Don't faint on me, buddy."

"I wouldn't dream of it."

Saunders hopped off the desk and poured Julian a glass of water. Numbly, Julian accepted it, noting how heavy the crystal was and how poorly his fingers were functioning.

Saunders took the glass away and faced him. He was wearing his sternest, most intimidating lawyer face. "I will take this reaction as a big yes to the possibility-of-issue question."

Julian swallowed, or tried to. "It may be okay."

"May?"

"Dee Ann might have, uh, taken care of things from her end."

"Julian, you sound like a teenager." Saunders crossed his arms. "You also sound as though you *didn't* 'take care of things.'"

Julian got to his feet and paced. "How could I have been so..." He flung up his arms.

"Stupid? Irresponsible?" Saunders began to pace, as well. "Immature? Lust-driven?"

"Drunk." They met in the center of Julian's office, passed each other, turned and met again. "This has never happened to me before," Julian said, heading for the door. "I've got to talk to Dee Ann."

"Wait a minute." Saunders stopped him. "These situations require the utmost delicacy and tact."

"I'm aware of that!" Julian rounded on him. "What did you think I was going to do? Go, hey, babe, you aren't knocked up or anything, are you?"

"I know you better than that. Or thought I did," Saunders muttered. "Before you broach the subject with Dee Ann, you should anticipate her responses both negatively or affirmatively and plan accordingly."

"Gad, Saunders, speak English, will you?"

"I can be your friend or your attorney. I can't be both at the same time." Saunders sniffed.

Julian was about to take a crack at the legal profession, but restrained himself. Saunders was right. He should have alternate plans. "Okay. If there is a possibility that there is a possibility, you know—" he gestured "—then I'll offer marriage." He looked to Saunders for acknowledgment.

"That might not be necessary."

"Saunders! If the woman is pregnant with my child, of course I'll offer marriage."

"You misunderstand—although it would be somewhat irregular, the ceremony performed last night could be construed as legally binding."

"Give me a break. Roy is a lawyer, not a priest."

"Roy is a justice of the peace, as of last November's elections." Saunders stepped back after dropping his bombshell.

"Oh, Lord, I'd forgotten that."

"How could you? He's worked it into every conversation for months."

Julian broke out in a sweat, something he rarely did. His headache, which had never completely abated, pounded anew. "Are you telling me that I might actually be *married* to Dee Ann?"

"Well, Roy seems to have misplaced the license and hasn't filed it yet." Saunders gave a weak laugh. "I was supposed to find a way to break the news to you. Since you're so hung up on possible fatherhood, I thought I'd sneak this in now."

Julian took a deep, cleansing breath as relief made his knees weak. He collapsed on the Italian-leather sofa lining the wall. "And if the license isn't filed, the wedding's not legal, right?"

"There wouldn't be any record of it."

"Thank you, Dee Ann!" Julian brought his fingers to his lips and kissed them.

"Why?"

"In a gesture as grand as any I've ever seen, she tore the thing to bits and flung it out to sea."

Saunders frowned. "She may regret that. She could still sue you for breach."

"Let's not worry about that now," Julian began.

"Worry about what?" Carter and Nikki came into the room.

"Oh, stuff." Julian shot Saunders a warning look. Saunders responded with an aggrieved expression. He hated it when anyone questioned his legal integrity, Julian knew.

"Here's a loan from petty cash until you can replace your bank card." Carter handed Julian a packet of bills.

"I won't need all this," Julian protested.

"Don't get excited, they're mostly ones." Nikki linked her arm through Carter's. "Good luck, Julian. I'd offer to help, but I'm afraid you'd take me up on it and right now, I'm dragging my husband off for our honeymoon."

"Oh, gee," Julian said in mock protest, "don't you want to stay and see us on the news?"

They shook their heads. "We're making a break for the *Honey Bee* and going far, far away." Carter smiled at his wife.

"I'd advise you to do likewise." Nikki chuckled. Then the two newlyweds were gone.

Julian heard them talking with someone in the hall a few seconds before Dee Ann poked her head in the doorway. "Security was calling for Carter. Something about a delivery from Margaux's?"

"Ah, dinner. Come in, Dee Ann." He grabbed the telephone, buzzed security and told them to send up the meal.

"I took the liberty of ordering a civilized dinner for us," he said, conscious that he was speaking too fast and too heartily.

"From Margaux's?" She looked pleased. "It's one of my favorite restaurants."

"And mine." Julian stared as Dee Ann shyly walked into his office.

She was wearing his pajamas.

She looked...incredible. He hoped she hadn't believed his story about wearing them in public. Her feet were bare, and her hair was still damp. She'd cuffed the sleeves and pants legs, but was still swallowed in yards of paisley silk which rippled when she moved. Somehow, she managed to look both adorable and enticing at the same time. A different enticing than in the *Honey Bee* bikini, but just as powerful.

Julian swallowed.

"Dinner was a great idea." Saunders had started

clearing off the coffee table in front of the sofa. "I'm starved."

"You aren't invited," Julian stated firmly. He'd forgotten all about Saunders.

Saunders straightened. "I *should* be," he said with a significant look toward Dee Ann.

"We've taken up too much of your personal time already." Julian clapped him on the shoulder and tried to steer him out the door.

Saunders dug in his heels. "Yes," he said distinctly. "Especially since I was in the middle of issuing a legal opinion."

"So you'll want to get back to it." Julian pushed harder.

"I certainly do," Saunders gripped the desk for leverage. "I wasn't finished."

"Julian," Dee Ann broke in as a knock sounded on the door, "the portions at Margaux's are so generous, I know there'll be enough to share with Saunders. It seems only right after we spoiled his Sunday afternoon."

"Oh, you didn't spoil it," Saunders said with a huge grin. "I wouldn't have missed this for any—*ouch!*"

"Julian, please." Dee Ann said as she walked over to open the door for the delivery boy.

While she was overseeing the table setting, Julian alternated between glaring at the smugly victorious Saunders and at the delivery boy, who was ogling Dee Ann. She seemed oblivious to the fact that the pajama lapels had a tendency to gape open. "We'll finish up ourselves," Julian said, reaching for the packet of bills, hoping there was at least one twenty.

"Oh, no, sir, I'm to—"

"As far as we're concerned, your service has been exemplary." Julian found a twenty and poked it into the boy's pocket. He signed the delivery bill, adding another gratuity, and showed the beaming teenager to the door.

If only Saunders could be disposed of as easily.

Saunders was worried that Julian would legally entangle himself or make promises he'd later regret, he knew. Even so, Julian's role in Dee Ann's possible pregnancy was something he wanted to discuss with her in private.

Not once had she brought up the subject, so Julian knew it was up to him. He hoped the omission on her part was a sign that there would be no reminders of their cruise nine months hence.

He watched as she and Saunders finished turning his office sitting area into an impromptu dining room.

"Good grief, Julian, did you order an entire cow?" Saunders gazed at two plates with massive cuts of bleeding prime rib.

"I suppose I sounded hungry over the telephone," Julian said, reluctantly accepting Saunders as their dinner companion.

"Let's see, I can use the bread-and-butter plate and leave you the dinner plate," Dee Ann said to the lawyer. "We'll have to share the knife, but I can use the dessert fork."

His fence-mending goodwill dinner was being ruined by Saunders. Dee Ann was offering to share, thus drawing her and Saunders closer and leaving Julian to appear selfish and inconsiderate. Look at them sitting on the couch, laughing together as if they didn't have a care in the world, he thought grimly.

This was not his plan. His plan was to foster a pleasant atmosphere and tie up a few loose ends in a mature manner. At least he and Dee Ann could part amicably, he hoped.

As Saunders and Dee Ann contentedly shared her dinner, Julian watched morosely. He didn't even bother to uncork the bottle of burgundy he kept in the bar. Burgundy bottled that year should properly breathe for twenty-two minutes, anyway.

"Julian, aren't you hungry?" Dee Ann asked, at last noticing him.

He managed a smile. "Famished." Picking up his knife, he cut into his meat. "I was just thinking how civilized we're all managing to be."

Dee Ann shrugged. "I can't change what happened. I'm as much to blame for this situation as you and I'd like to put everything behind us."

"Excellent," Saunders managed to say around a mouthful of prime rib. "I congratulate you both on accepting equal responsibility."

Julian kicked him under the table. He knew Saunders was covering Julian for a lawsuit later. But still, how unsubtle could he get?

Apparently, Dee Ann didn't see any ulterior motives in Saunders's comments and chattered away as if she were at one of the many business dinners they both attended during the year. Julian admired her remarkable sangfroid, though he couldn't help contrasting it to her behavior on the *Honey Bee*.

Here it was, just after ten o'clock at night and she wasn't showing any signs of wanting to return home. Granted, they were waiting out the press and he'd offered dinner, but she hadn't asked about clothes, seemed unconcerned about transportation and had no money, as far as he knew. He was prepared to help, but it was curious that she hadn't even broached the subject.

And then he understood and relaxed. Dee Ann was using Saunders as a buffer. She didn't want to be alone with him.

Well, Saunders wouldn't stay here all night, Julian thought, eating his dinner with renewed appetite.

Dee Ann and Saunders were splitting her piece of chocolate-raspberry-truffle cheesecake, when the telephone rang.

Saunders leaped up to answer it and Julian let him. He had to speak privately to Dee Ann. But before he could maneuver a conversation, gracefully working in the more troublesome aspects of their situation, Saunders dropped the phone and ran out of the office.

"Saunders?" Julian called.

The lawyer didn't answer.

Dee Ann and Julian stared at each other, then hurried after him.

They found him in the conference room, staring at a television set. Against a background of grainy newspaper photos of the Beldens, an earnest newscaster was leading into the story.

"Oh, no!" Dee Ann covered her mouth with her hands.

"Shh! I'm listening for slander," Saunders said as he scribbled down notes.

Tape of Julian and Dee Ann running for Carter's car played as the voice-over put the day's events in the worst possible light.

There was considerable footage of Saunders saying "No comment" and looking harassed.

Dee Ann had pulled up her T-shirt up to cover her face and in the process, had exposed her legs.

Julian looked like a bum, but a bum with a good haircut.

"And the honeymooning Beldens are unavailable for comment," concluded the reporter.

The station news anchor followed this with Dee Ann's engagement photos and that story. There was even a two-year-old picture of Julian, obviously gleaned from the newspaper society pages.

Dee Ann collapsed onto her knees in front of the TV as the next story began. "They didn't say the charges were dropped, did they, Saunders?"

The lawyer quickly reviewed his notes. "Yes, but in such a way that it sounded like they shouldn't have been." He shook his head. "Nothing here, folks. They were very careful."

The phone rang.

"Don't answer it," Saunders ordered.

"I have to call my parents," Dee Ann mumbled and stood up on visibly shaking legs.

Julian felt just as shaken. He'd been expecting this, but to watch it, knowing all of Galveston was seeing the story, knowing Houston stations had undoubtedly picked it up, as well, was a blow to his usual aplomb.

"Wait." Saunders pulled out the conference-room chairs. "You sit here." He positioned Dee Ann and nodded to the chair next to her.

Julian took it with an encouraging smile at Dee Ann. It was an empty smile, but he felt honor-bound to make the attempt. "Saunders is in lawyer mode. Just go along with him."

"About that," Saunders began, settling himself against the conference table in front of them. "Dee Ann, am I representing you in this matter?"

She nodded.

"Then as your attorney, I advise you to speak to no one until we formulate your statements."

"But my mother—"

"Especially your mother," Julian interrupted.

When Dee Ann looked as though she was about to object, Saunders held up his hand. "Your mother will be speaking with her friends. I'll contact her and tell her that you're okay."

"Tell her...tell her that I've gone to Rocky Falls to visit Grandmother," Dee Ann said.

"You're going to run away?" Julian asked.

Dee Ann faced him with a defiant tilt to her chin. "I've recently acquired property in Rocky Falls. This is an excellent time to inspect it."

The phone rang again. Julian had a sudden vision of ringing phones, faxes, sly remarks and microphones thrust in his face. "Great idea, Dee Ann. I'm coming with you."

6

"THAT WON'T BE necessary, Julian." Dee Ann wanted to get away from everyone—especially Julian. The strain of being civil was taking its toll. She stood, with the intention of leaving the conference room, locking herself in Carter's office and punching a few pillows. Then she was going to make anonymous phone calls to the local media with titillating, but erroneous, news tips.

"Oh, but I insist." Julian fairly leaped to his feet. "I became quite enamored of Rocky Falls during my brief sojourn there."

"Really." Dee Ann leveled a skeptical look at Julian, which he met with equanimity. "I would have thought Rocky Falls was too rural for you."

"Rural holds a certain appeal right now." His gaze dipped as Dee Ann felt the pajama lapels slither apart. She pretended she didn't notice rather than let him know he affected her one way or the other.

"I'll come, too." Saunders slid off the table.

"No!" Dee Ann and Julian shouted at him in unison. Saunders managed to look cowed and determinedly stubborn at the same time.

"I think it would be best if we went our separate ways." Dee Ann gripped the lapels closed. "Isn't there a small European country you'd like to visit?"

"August is a terrible month to travel in Europe." Julian cleared his throat. "Besides, I wouldn't feel right abandoning you at this, ah...juncture." During his brief hesitation, he'd glanced at Saunders as if for confirmation.

"What juncture?" she asked.

He raised his eyebrows. "We're the main course at a media banquet, for one thing."

"And for another?"

She'd been speaking to Julian, but Saunders replied. "The consequences of the past twenty-four hours haven't been fully explored."

What? Dee Ann tried to read their expressions. Did they think she was going to sue? That she'd want to attract even *more* attention to herself by dragging everything out in court? Not after the summer she'd had.

Besides, who would she sue? The police? The Coast Guard? They were just doing their jobs. The Beldens? They'd thought their boat had been stolen. And, actually, it had been. She and Julian had stolen it.

Could she sue Julian? Perhaps, but Dee Ann still couldn't remember much of the previous night, so how could she accuse him of any wrongdoing? In fact, there was overwhelming evidence that she'd been a willing participant in their revelry.

She looked at him now, while he was in elegant profile, busy glaring at Saunders. She sighed at the perfection of Julian's nose—God-given, she was certain—and her heart gave a funny blip. If only...

If only they could start all over. But they couldn't and the sooner she escaped, the better. "As far as I'm concerned," she announced, drawing their attention back to her, "the incident is over. Let's just consider it one of life's character builders and leave it at that."

"But the press," Saunders began.

"Will soon find other victims," she stated. And she wasn't planning to stick around for any in-depth interviews. "You've both been too kind and I've trespassed on your hospitality long enough." As she mouthed a few more conventional phrases, Dee Ann edged toward the door.

"Not at all," Julian protested too firmly. "Don't feel you have to rush away. On the other hand, Saunders, it *is* getting late."

"Exactly," Dee Ann said. "So I'll say good-night." She included both of them and started out the door.

"No, wait." Julian stepped in front of her. "Would you like a cup of coffee—or tea? You prefer tea, don't you?"

Julian was ruining her exit. His dinner had been a graceful end to the debacle; Dee Ann couldn't believe he was overplaying his hand this way. It was very unlike the Julian she knew.

Since she, Julian and the Beldens moved in the same business and social circles, it was inevitable that they'd run into each other in the future. After all the publicity generated by the *Honey Bee* fiasco, their public encounters would be watched avidly, then dissected for signs of malice and strain. Right now, in spite of the past twenty-four hours, Dee Ann felt she could look the Belden bunch in the face and not cringe. She wanted to keep it that way. Julian should let well enough alone.

The intercom buzzed and Saunders answered it. "Security says the phone lines are jammed," he reported.

"Tell them to let voice mail deal with it," Julian snapped, then waved his hand. "Sorry." Apparently, he wasn't as unaffected by the situation as she supposed. Turning to her, he spoke in an undertone, "I wanted the opportunity to speak with you privately."

Enough. There had been enough apologies, enough explanations. "Julian, don't worry. I have no intention of ever referring to the past twenty-four hours again. You have behaved with the utmost discretion and I appreciate it." She glared at Saunders, who was scribbling furiously. "Shall I repeat that, or did you manage to get it all down?"

"No, it was lovely, though if you could just add a phrase about—"

"Saunders!" Julian looked ready to explode.

Dee Ann placed a restraining hand on his arm and felt his muscles tighten. "I understand, Julian. We live in a litigious society. Saunders is just trying to cover all the possibilities."

"Since Julian failed to cover himself at a crucial moment last night," Saunders muttered as he took notes.

"Saunders, *please*," Julian whispered, his eyes closed, his expression pained.

"What about last night?" Dee Ann tried to fit the fragmented pieces she could remember into a coherent picture. "Is he talking about the wedding license?"

"Not exactly." Julian ushered her out the door of the conference room. "We can discuss it all on the way to Rocky Falls tomorrow. *When we're alone*," he said over his shoulder at Saunders. "For now, I think we can all use a good night's sleep." With his hand on the small of her back, Julian urged her down the hallway. "The sofa in Carter's office unfolds to a bed. Sheets and pillows should be in the linen closet in the bathroom—"

"What is Saunders talking about?" Dee Ann turned in the doorway of Carter's office and faced Julian.

To his credit, Julian quit trying to distract her. He gazed into space for a moment, then spoke, "When Saunders mentioned covering myself, he wasn't speaking symbolically." Julian looked directly into her eyes. "We need to discuss the possibility of a pregnancy—your pregnancy."

Pregnant. She inhaled sharply. So that was it. They were worried that she might be pregnant. Dee Ann's heart sped up and she licked her suddenly dry lips. She'd never even considered... Pregnant! Preg-*nant*. Preg-*nant*. Her heart beat in rhythm with the word. She brought her hand to her temple. "I could be pregnant?" she asked, hearing her voice sound high and breathy.

"I certainly did my part."

Dee Ann closed her eyes. "I don't really remember..."

"How mortifying," was his dry comment.

Her eyes flew open and she felt compelled to reassure him. "Oh, no, Julian, I'm certain you were...were *fine*."

He exhaled. "But hardly memorable."

Men had such fragile egos in the performance arena. It was gratifying to see that the sophisticated Julian was no different. "That's not your fault. I obviously wasn't at my best."

"Oh, no," he said softly. "You were sublime."

"Don't you mean comatose?"

He chuckled. "Naturally, the first time there was the usual getting-acquainted awkwardness—"

"The *first* time?"

"—but the second..." Wearing a private smile, Julian sighed. "Ecstasy."

"Ecstasy?" Dee Ann wished she could remember some of it.

"Mmm." With a shake of his head, he refocused on her. "I don't think we need to count the third time."

"The th—" She felt heat wash over her body. "Why not?"

He raised an eyebrow. "You can't get pregnant that way."

Her eyes widened. She wasn't going to ask. He was probably making this up, or part of it, anyway. Three times. In his dreams. "So, not counting round three, I might be pregnant." She felt numb—but not devastated. Probably because she still couldn't remember anything.

"Unless you're using some form of birth control, it's definitely a possibility." And one Julian didn't sound thrilled about, she noted. But that would be asking an awful lot of him—of any man in this situation.

"I want children." She looked up at him. "Carter and I were going to start a family right away." And she'd mourned that loss more than her broken wedding. "So, no, I wasn't using birth control."

"I see." Julian stared into her eyes, then drew her close. Through the silk pajamas—his pajamas—she could feel the warmth of his arms. For a brief moment, she allowed herself to dream of discussing a pregnancy the way it should have been discussed—with her husband. Making plans. Trying out names.

But Dee Ann Karrenbrock didn't have a husband. And now she might be faced with either becoming an unwed mother, or having a shotgun wedding, assuming Julian would offer marriage. Wouldn't that be lovely? Everyone in Galveston would count on their fingers—and come up short. She shuddered.

"It'll be all right, Dee Ann," Julian said soothingly, his voice rumbling against her ear. "I won't let you go through this alone. I'm staying with you until we know one way or the other."

DEE ANN did not sleep well that night. Lying on the sofa bed in the office of a man to whom she'd once been engaged, wearing the pajamas of another man—whose child she might be carrying—Dee Ann wrestled with her thoughts. The only conclusion she reached was that she didn't want to hear Julian offer her marriage. He would, she knew, because offering marriage was the honorable course to take.

But Dee Ann still had her pride. She refused to accept a proposal of marriage that was forced by circumstances.

Of course, if the license she'd torn up was any indication, she'd not only accepted Julian's proposal, she'd actually married him. And had had quite a honeymoon, it seemed. If necessary, to satisfy the finger-counters, she and Julian could acknowledge last night's ceremony. A discreet announcement with that date...

What was she thinking?

Last night was a mistake. Several mistakes. Apparently, at least three.

Forcing Julian into marriage, however much he claimed to be willing, would be another. She couldn't do it. She *wouldn't* do it.

Just before dawn, Dee Ann gave up trying to sleep and raided Carter's closet. She hit pay dirt with a T-shirt and elastic-waisted jogging shorts. Without any hesitation whatsoever, Dee Ann also borrowed Carter's jogging shoes. How mortifying to discover that they weren't as huge on her as she thought they were going to be. Still, they were big enough. She hoped she wouldn't have to walk far.

Pulling her hair into a messy ponytail, she sneaked out of Carter's office.

Julian's door was closed and Dee Ann left his pajamas folded neatly on the floor outside.

The night security guard was getting off his shift and gave her a ride to the hotel parking lot where she'd left her car.

Unfortunately, as the guard drove away, Dee Ann realized she had no car keys. No driver's license. No purse. No house keys. No money.

Dawn was a rosy idea on the eastern horizon as Dee Ann pondered her situation. There was no choice, really. She was going to have to ask the hotel concierge for help. Feeling self-conscious, she trudged toward the palm-lined entrance of one of Galveston's finest hotels.

Sand got in her—Carter's—shoes. She wore no socks.

She wore no underwear.

And everyone would probably be able to tell.

It was funny how each day brought some new form of humiliation with it.

As she was about to lose her nerve, a couple dressed in similar attire to hers jogged down the steps and along the tiled path toward her. As they passed, they nodded, apparently considering her a fellow early-morning jogger.

Dee Ann picked up speed, as much as she could in the large shoes, bounded up the stairs and over to the concierge, who gazed at her impassively from behind a dark wooden desk.

She drew a couple of deep breaths to keep up the jogger image and announced, "I'm Dee Ann Karrenbrock—"

"One moment." The man stood and went to the bank of brass mailboxes behind him.

He thought she was a guest at the hotel and was checking for messages. Or he was alerting the media. Dee Ann was just about to call to him, when he plucked a paper from one of the boxes and disappeared around the corner.

Nervously, she glanced over her shoulder, but no one seemed the least bit interested in her. And more important, no one seemed to connect her to the bedraggled woman on last night's news.

A few minutes later, the concierge reappeared carrying a sandy, water-stained, pale blue lump.

"My purse!" A miracle. Fate must have taken pity on her.

"Yes, ma'am. The caterers found it as they cleaned the beach."

Astonished, Dee Ann pried open the already rusting clasp.

"I'm afraid the saltwater has ruined the leather, but the contents appear to be intact," the concierge intoned virtuously.

Inside, damp and sandy, was her wallet—and her keys. Hardly daring to believe her good fortune, Dee Ann unsnapped her wallet, shaking sand all over the dark wooden perfection of the concierge's desk.

Everything in her wallet was still there. Her money. Her credit cards. Her driver's license. She was free!

Leaving the concierge a generous, but slightly damp, tip, Dee Ann let him know she was taking her car and that Julian would probably arrive shortly for his. Then she raced out the front door.

Home. She was going home.

Dee Ann had nearly arrived before she remembered the reporters. Would they still be there? Had her tip been big enough or would the concierge alert them?

With trepidation, she turned onto her street and slammed on the brakes.

A lone van with a satellite dish on top was parked in front of her house.

It was past dawn, though still early, and Monday-morning commuter traffic would soon pick up. She had to make her move now or lose the opportunity.

It was risky, but Dee Ann didn't care. She decided to

make a run for it, pack as fast as she could and head for Rocky Falls. Even if the reporters followed her, how long could the television station afford to devote an entire remote unit to pursuing her across Texas?

As a businesswoman, Dee Ann knew pursuing her wouldn't be cost-effective. Assuming the station manager would come to that conclusion, as well, she put her car in gear and drove slowly down the street.

Once again, luck was with her. She pulled into her driveway with no movement from within the van. The reporters must have fallen asleep.

The garage was empty, which meant her parents weren't at home and probably hadn't been all night. That explained why she hadn't been able to reach them. And what a relief to avoid explaining everything to them right now, she thought as she scurried from the garage to her house.

Fingers shaking, Dee Ann unlocked her back door and slipped inside.

She was safe.

For now.

"WHAT MAKES YOU so sure she didn't go directly to Rocky Falls?" Saunders asked from inside Julian's closet.

Julian looked up from his packing. "If she did, then you can drive me there."

Saunders flipped the switch that marched Julian's suits past him. It was the fourth time he'd done so. "Now, Julian, buddy, I don't mind the driver's-license paperwork or replacing your credit cards, but come on, I've got work to do."

Julian smiled without humor. "Carter gave the staff two weeks off."

"Which I plan to use to catch up."

Julian zipped his leather satchel. "You'll never catch up, Saunders."

"Not with your escapades, I won't. Speaking of which, shall I draw up papers in the event of—"

"She's not going to sue."

"Maybe not now—"

"She'll have no need," Julian stated. He intended to be married to the mother of his child when that child was born, period.

"Okay, okay." Saunders emerged from the closet and headed toward the exercise equipment in the corner.

He'd probably hurt himself if Julian didn't distract him. "Grab the hanging bag, will you?" Julian nodded toward it and swung his satchel over his shoulder.

Saunders willingly abandoned his wanderings. "However will you amuse yourself in a little place like Rocky Falls, Texas?"

Julian thought of the Dee Ann he'd discovered in the past two days and smiled. "I'll find a way."

LOST IN A FRENZY of packing, Dee Ann didn't hear the pounding on her back door at first. Then, assuming it was reporters, she ignored it.

"Dee Ann?" The voice sounded muffled but familiar.

It couldn't be Julian.

But, of course, it was.

"Go away!" she shouted from the top of the stairs.

"Dee Ann, let me in. I want to talk with you."

How had he found her so quickly? "I *don't* want to talk with you."

"But you're going to have to sometime."

"Make it some *other* time."

"Open the door," he commanded, sounding not at all like the usually diplomatic Julian she knew. This was a determined Julian.

Looking for a way to escape, Dee Ann eyed her bedroom window. She hadn't been able to climb through it when she was young, so she certainly couldn't now. Her only hope was that the reporters would overwhelm him and he'd have to leave.

"Dee Ann Karrenbrock, open this door!"

"Julian, you do realize the reporters will hear you." She held her breath.

"Let them hear." Julian accompanied this with more pounding. "I'm not leaving until we've settled things."

If he didn't stop it, he'd break down the door.

Surrendering, Dee Ann ran down the stairs and jerked open the door. "What do you want?"

Julian pushed his way inside. "You knew I wanted to talk with you, yet you snuck out like a thief this morning."

Dee Ann raised her chin belligerently. "You were asleep."

"Hardly." He ran a hand through his hair.

She would have argued the point, but she could see the tiredness in his eyes. She could imagine what thoughts had kept him awake. Something on the order of sacrificing his carefree bachelor life to honor.

Well, she wasn't having any of it. She'd rather have no husband than a reluctant one. She turned to go upstairs. "If you want to talk, talk now. I'm leaving for Rocky Falls as soon as I get my suitcase packed."

He was right behind her. "And I told you I was coming with you."

"Drop it, Julian."

"No."

Dee Ann turned back briefly, met his determined gray gaze, shrugged a shoulder and continued up the stairs. She wouldn't argue with him now. "Where's Saunders? I'm surprised he's not here making sure you don't incriminate yourself."

"He dropped me off and went to see about my car."

"I saw it this morning. It looked okay."

"Dee Ann, I don't want to talk about my car. I want to discuss your plans."

"My only plans are to get out of here without ending up on the six o'clock news!"

They were at the entrance to her bedroom—her childhood bedroom with a four-poster bed done in innocent white eyelet, with tiny purple violets wallpapered everywhere, even on the ceiling. She'd always loved this room when she was a child, but thought she'd outgrown it. Yet, during the summer weeks after being jilted by Carter, she'd found the familiar room comforting as she slipped back into the routine of being the daughter of the house.

And now the daughter of the house had a man in her

bedroom. As he stepped inside, an alien presence framed by the white canopy, she saw Julian's gaze sweep the room and wondered what he was thinking. Wondered if he felt as awkward as she suddenly did.

In all the years she'd spent growing up in this house, Dee Ann had never had a boy, let alone a man, in her bedroom. It just wasn't done. She'd entertained men when she'd been living on her own, but this was different. This was her parents' house. For some reason, she felt more vulnerable here and was keenly aware that her parents would disapprove of Julian being in her room.

Trying to shake the feeling, Dee Ann returned to her haphazard packing.

"Have you thought—"

"No!" Dee Ann stuffed her underwear into the suitcase and slammed it shut. "I don't even know if I'm pregnant yet." She hurried past him into the bathroom and began dumping cosmetics into her travel case.

He stood in the doorway; she could see his shadow on the white sink. "I'm offering my support for whatever decision you choose to make."

Dee Ann met his eyes in the mirror. His expression was calm and his smile was encouraging. He looked safe. Strong and dependable. And unbelievably handsome.

Dee Ann thought she was going to cry. Why was he being so decent? She didn't want him to be decent. She wanted to be angry with him. "Thank you," she managed to say.

"That includes marriage, Dee Ann."

The word *marriage* stabbed her in the heart. "*Why* did you say that?" She whirled and saw a look of complete bewilderment cross his face. "Don't answer." Grabbing the case and her hair dryer, she pushed past him.

"Dee Ann—"

"Don't. Just don't say anything." She zipped her cosmetics case shut and tried cramming it into the suitcase. Naturally, the suitcase wouldn't shut on the first try, so she stirred the contents and tried again, succeeding in fastening one side but not the other.

Good enough.

She was about to drag it off the bed, when Julian stopped her. Taking the suitcase, he set it on the bed and unfastened it.

"Julian, don't bother with that. I've got to get out of here." Dee Ann picked up a smaller suitcase containing nothing but shoes and business papers.

Ignoring her, Julian calmly refolded everything and shut the case with a loud click. Then he stood it on the floor and straddled the edge. "Ready to talk?"

"No."

He barely blinked.

Dee Ann had a bad feeling about this. "I promise to tell you the instant I know anything."

This made no impression at all on Julian.

"You're not going to give me that suitcase until you get your way, are you?"

"No."

"Very tricky maneuver, Julian," she acknowledged, unwillingly flattered by his persistence.

He grinned. Even his teeth were elegant.

Dee Ann couldn't stand it. Yes, she might be a fallen woman, but she'd been tripped up by the best. "Please. I don't want to get caught by the reporters." As if they weren't awake by now. "And if you think the press is bad, you haven't met my mother."

"Then we'll talk in the car."

"In the—you're not still insisting on going with me to Rocky Falls?"

"Yes, I am." His gaze was steely. "And my apologies, but you'll have to drive. I understand that the hotel found your purse, but my wallet remains a casualty."

He sat there, implacable. Precious minutes ticked away as Dee Ann stared at him, weighing which would be worse—facing the press and her mother—or having Julian in the car with her for three hours.

No contest. Besides, a couple of days in the country would send Julian right back to the city.

Of course, a couple of days in the country might send her back, as well.

"Okay, Julian. You win."

7

DEE ANN HAD NEVER realized how difficult making light conversation could be.

Or how entertaining.

Even Julian's mild flirting didn't annoy her the way she would have expected it to. It was all fake, but Julian could be so convincing, Dee Ann frequently forgot that she hadn't wanted him to come along.

The three-hour drive passed unexpectedly quickly. Julian was a charming companion. Not that Dee Ann was surprised, but what *did* surprise her was that he could maintain the pleasantries for so long. She wasn't any help until she realized how childish she was being. Pouting was very unlike her and it startled her to realize that pouting was exactly what she was doing. What had happened to her?

Giving herself a mental shake, she shouldered her half of the conversation. They tiptoed around the reason for their forced togetherness and engaged in light verbal skirmishes.

The drive out of Galveston was uneventful, but once in Houston, they managed to hit the very worst of the morning rush-hour traffic.

As they inched their way along clogged freeways, Julian started discussing the wine lists of the various

Houston restaurants. "The Bayou Court has an excellent cellar of reds."

"Fine, if you want to clog your arteries with all that heavy beef they serve."

"I'd rather risk clogging my arteries than assault my taste buds by drinking a watery white wine with a salad, the way women do."

"Not all whites are watery," Dee Ann protested, though she'd been guilty of the salad infraction. "And what if I happen to *prefer* white wine? And what if I want to drink it with a small serving of beef? Why can't I do so without some man who thinks he's superior making a crack about women and wines?"

This led to a pleasant squabble about the ultimate dinner and which wines should accompany each course.

Julian knew much more about wine than she did and by the time they cleared Houston, he'd recommended the names of so many wonderful wines that Dee Ann wanted to throw a small elegant dinner party every night for a few months.

Dee Ann was happily occupied in mental menu planning when they reached a highway intersection and she spotted a bright yellow billboard that read, Pregnant? Need Help? followed by a telephone number.

She tried to pretend she didn't see the sign, but they got caught at the traffic light underneath it.

"Good reminder," Julian said and searched her glove compartment. "May I write on your map?"

"What?"

"You don't have my home telephone number," he gestured to the sign. "It's unlisted."

Great. She might be having his child, but she didn't even have his telephone number.

While scribbling on her map, Julian launched into a discussion of restaurants with the best desserts, followed by a debate concerning the best exercises to burn off the calories, making Dee Ann quickly forget her embarrassment.

The only other awkward moment came when she pointed out the small Texas Hill Country Winery not far from Rocky Falls. They were three-quarters of the way into planning a weekend excursion before both of them realized what they were doing.

Dee Ann broke off abruptly and with a barely discernible sigh, Julian changed the subject, which lasted until they arrived.

"Here it is, beautiful downtown Rocky Falls," Dee Ann announced. "Look quick." A strip of stores that would be the perfect location for a black-and-white film noir about the fifties, staked its claim on either side of Rocky Falls's only four-lane street. Dee Ann slid a sideways look at Julian as she pulled into Otto's Garage and Snack Bar, a particularly unpicturesque establishment on the fringes of town.

"Why are we stopping here?" Julian asked. "Your grandmother's coffee shop isn't far, as I recall."

"We're stopping here *because* KK's isn't far. I want to get our story straight. Grandmother is going to wonder what I'm doing here with you."

"Why not just tell your grandmother the truth?" Julian suggested, shifting in the seat so he faced her.

The truth would require lengthy explanations. Besides, Dee Ann wasn't certain what the truth was anymore. "I'd hoped to spare her that."

He gave her a sympathetic smile. "Don't believe for a minute that she hasn't heard every salacious detail. We've been all over the news."

"*Galveston* news."

Julian leveled a look at her.

"Okay, and Houston news," Dee Ann conceded. "But people around here don't care what goes on in Galveston." After all, she didn't particularly care what happened in Rocky Falls, unless it concerned her grandmother.

Julian squinted at the front of Otto's. "Have you seen the papers this morning?"

The papers. More than one? "No...how bad is it?"

Julian glanced back at her. Dee Ann's blond hair hadn't been styled and was hanging in slight waves, just reaching below her chin. Her eyes were wide and she looked about ten years old, nothing like the long-legged bathing beauty who walked across the inside pages of every morning newspaper in the area.

Nor did she resemble the cool, surprisingly clever professional he'd encountered across the conference table during her takeover attempt of Carter's company. They'd all thought they were dealing with an aging debutante. Well, they were, but this aging debutante had an MBA and a killer instinct.

She would have won, too, if her ruthless businessman father hadn't exhibited an unfortunate sentimental streak.

Still, Victor Karrenbrock and his daughter had obviously made some enemies in their time and now those enemies were using their influence to convince the media that they had a scandal on their hands.

Then again, he and Carter Belden had made a few enemies, too.

This whole incident was being portrayed as the decadent rich getting what they deserved, and unfortunately, they were getting it on a slow news day. Where was a hurricane when you needed one?

"Wait here." He jumped out of the car and approached a red newspaper dispenser. Shoving in quarters, he grabbed a Houston paper. She needed to see exactly what the town had seen. What her grandmother had no doubt been shown.

When he got back inside the car, Julian opened the paper to their picture, the one with Dee Ann pulling the T-shirt over her face and exposing her legs. His borrowed swim trunks were cropped out of this photo, leaving him with a bare torso.

"I've said it before and I'll say it again—you've got great legs." He handed her the paper, not knowing exactly how she'd take his comment.

"Thank heavens," she murmured, scanning the picture without expression. "You're not so bad, yourself."

That surprised him and he shot her a startled look.

She intercepted it with a cool, "I don't think it's a secret that I find you attractive."

Julian wasn't often nonplussed, but he was now. This

was not the reaction he'd expected and he couldn't figure out what had prompted it. "You're taking this surprisingly well," he mentioned cautiously.

Dee Ann threw back her head and laughed. Julian had never seen her laugh that way, either. He regarded her warily.

When she saw his expression, Dee Ann laughed again, for far too long, in Julian's opinion. "You don't know what to think, do you?" she asked.

"No, but I'm thinking hysteria."

She sobered, gesturing to the newspaper. "Actually, I was dreading this, but you know what?"

Julian shook his head.

"What more can they print? We're both here, the Beldens are honeymooning, the charges were dropped... there's nothing left to report." She sighed and gripped the steering wheel. "But what do I tell my grandmother?"

"Tell her that I'm your fiancé."

"No."

"Why not?"

She studied him as though he were an acquisition she might add to her stock portfolio. "I'm not going to lie to my grandmother."

"It doesn't have to be a lie," Julian found himself saying. Where had that come from? As the words soaked into the silence inside Dee Ann's car, Julian didn't know who was more surprised by his suggestion.

Or more wary.

Dee Ann folded the newspaper, aligning the creases and smoothing the paper as though she planned to save it for her scrapbook. "No," she said at last, not meeting his eyes.

Julian waved away the mechanic who approached them. "Why not?" he asked.

Dee Ann leaned against the headrest. "Back in Galveston, you're known as a guy who's great to date between boyfriends, but everyone knows you have no interest in marriage."

"People change."

"But you haven't." She rolled her head until she met his gaze. "I thought you might have when you asked me out last winter. But you made it very clear you weren't interested in a long-term commitment."

He nodded. "And you made it just as clear that you were."

"So why did you ask me out again?"

Well, for sex, but he couldn't say that. "Why did you agree to go out with me?"

Something flickered in her eyes. "Because of your nose."

"What?"

She laughed. "You've seen my grandmother. You've seen my father. With a nose like that in the family, a girl can't be too careful when she selects her children's father."

Julian was flabbergasted. "Your nose looks okay."

"*Now* it does." She presented her profile to him. "Mom started my nose fund when I was born, just in case."

"You're kidding." Julian studied Dee Ann's nose. It wasn't the tiny tip-tilted one favored by cheerleaders, nor was it even particularly small. He would have never guessed that her nose wasn't a complete work of nature.

She pointed to the side. "Both my grandmother and my father had the same twisted hump with a bony knob inside. It caused all sorts of sinus problems. They've both had surgery. When it was my turn, I had a little extra done, too. We weren't trying to change the way I looked, so much as bring everything into balance. But still, I missed out on an entire summer of fun when I was in high school." She gave an exaggerated sigh. "When I agreed to go out with you, I was only trying to spare my children that."

Julian pulled down the sun visor and studied his reflection in the vanity mirror. He'd never really noticed his nose before. "I don't understand the subtle difference between your being eager to add me to your family's gene pool last winter—and as recently as several days ago—but not now."

"Because you wouldn't be considering marriage if you didn't think I might be pregnant."

"And what better time to consider marriage?" Julian said with an attempt at lightness. It sounded lame even to him. "Dee Ann," he said when she didn't respond, "we'll never know how our relationship might have progressed."

She sat upright. "It wasn't going anywhere! *I*—" she jabbed at herself "—remember that conversation. You asked me why I wasn't working for my father anymore and I told you that I was ready to settle down and start a family, that I was looking forward to having children and wanted to stay at home with them when they were small. All I had to say was the word *children* and you shuddered, Julian. *Shuddered.*"

"Involuntary reaction."

"But very telling." She shook her head. "I knew then it was hopeless, and so I moved on."

"It would have been nice if you'd waited to move on until *after* the date."

"Oh, for heaven's sake! It was a *business* reception, not a date. And I've already apologized." She started the car, shifting gears with irritation. "We'll just tell my grandmother that the whole mess was a misunderstanding that was blown out of proportion."

"I only thought that if you *are* pregnant, it would come as less of a shock to your grandmother if we'd already presented ourselves as an engaged couple."

Just before Dee Ann drove out into the street, she glanced over at him. "And if I'm not pregnant, what then? Another broken engagement on my record?"

Julian gazed into her icy blue eyes and felt chilled. Except for his renegade suggestion back there, he'd taken it for granted that if Dee Ann weren't pregnant, there would be no need for a wedding. It had never occurred to him that she might not feel the same way.

Dee Ann was insulted. Rightly so, Julian acknowledged, feeling like the bitter dregs left from a decanted bottle of burgundy.

He had botched this whole situation. Thoroughly.

But maybe, just maybe, not irretrievably.

FIANCÉE. Julian Wainright thought he was such a catch that she'd be glad, no, *grateful* to be his fiancée. That she was such a pitiful female that no one else would marry her in her condition—whatever it might be. For all she knew, he probably had the divorce planned, as well.

Forget it. She had no intention of foisting a reluctant father on her child.

Or a reluctant husband on herself.

Julian hadn't answered her question, which was an answer in itself, Dee Ann thought as she turned onto Main Street.

KK's Koffee Shoppe was on the right-hand side, situated between Louise's Laundry and Main Street Drugs. People would stop in while they waited on their laundry or while their prescriptions were being filled. Katrina Karrenbrock's coffee cake was a staple on the diets of nearly everyone in Rocky Falls.

And nearly everyone in Rocky Falls seemed to be parked on Main Street right now, Dee Ann decided, studying the slanted cars that bristled out from both sides of the street.

"Lunchtime," Julian commented.

"Yes." Dee Ann hit the brakes as a woman carrying a load of laundry walked to her car.

Within moments, the woman pulled out and Dee Ann nabbed her spot. "Let me do the talking, okay?" Without waiting for an answer, she got out of the car and slammed the door.

This was going to be tricky. Should she breeze in as if nothing was wrong, or should she quit pretending? What if the coffee shop's customers recognized her?

Dee Ann stood by the parking meter as she considered the best approach, something she should have done already instead of chatting with Julian all the way from Galveston.

A faded brown coffee cup with silvery-gray steam stuck out from the side of the building. KK's Koffee Shoppe curved around the saucer in an old-fashioned script. At night, neon lighting outlined the steam, the cup and saucer and the lettering, assuming it all lit up at the same time. Most of the time, some of the lights were burned out, leaving part of the sign black, thus rendering a surreal illustration of a coffee cup. Other times, the lights would flicker nervously. When that occurred, the people inside looked as if they were in a rock video.

It was awful.

And she owned it.

And Louise's Laundry. And the drugstore.

Julian took her elbow. "Come on. You've got to go in sometime." He looked at her and winked, then nodded toward the picture windows. "People are watching you."

They were, Dee Ann saw, with a sinking sensation in the pit of her stomach.

Or was that the effects of early pregnancy? was her other cheerful thought.

Julian opened the door, and the bell, the stupid cowbell her grandmother insisted on leaving up, clanked.

People stopped eating and drinking to stare; they didn't even try to hide it. Dee Ann was obviously a scarlet woman in the eyes of the inhabitants of Rocky Falls.

She heard a low murmur from behind her.

"Smile." Julian nudged her into the room.

He was right. "Hello, everybody!" Dee Ann smiled and waved, then headed for the kitchen, Julian in tow.

"Dee Ann!" Her short, German grandmother's mouth looked like a day-old doughnut.

The two elderly women with Katrina stared, then put their heads together and whispered.

Good grief. "Hi, yes, it's me." Dee Ann approached her grandmother and hugged the startled woman.

"Dee Ann, what is all this?" her grandmother asked, then apparently saw Julian for the first time and broke into German.

Dee Ann could only translate every third or fourth word, but then it wasn't necessary, was it? Julian had been recognized as her companion in shame. "Grandmother, this is Julian Wainright."

"I know. He bought my shop before you did." At least she was speaking English again. "How do you do, Mr. Wainright?"

Julian gave her a small bow and an easy smile. "Delighted to see you again, Mrs. Karrenbrock. And hoping for a piece of that marvelous coffee cake."

At least that's the gist of what he said. Since he spoke in a respectable German, Dee Ann wasn't exactly sure.

"Psh." Dimpling, Katrina waved both hands at him, then planted them on her ample hips. "Are you two, eh...?" She gestured from one to the other with her finger.

"No!" Dee Ann burst out.

"Yes," Julian said at the same time.

They glared at each other while Katrina clucked her tongue. "Like that, is it?"

"No." Dee Ann started to explain, but it was difficult because Julian slipped his arm around her waist and grinned a sappy I'm-in-love grin.

Katrina clapped her pudgy hands and beamed at the two women who had been watching the exchange avidly.

"You'll pay," Dee Ann threatened under her breath.

"Gladly," Julian whispered and planted a kiss next to her ear.

"Dee Ann..." Smiling, her grandmother held out her arms until Dee Ann hugged her again. "Come, sit." She beckoned them to the huge wooden table in the back where she made strudel in the winter. "I must finish lunch, then I want to hear all about what the papers said."

Without asking, Katrina brought them sandwiches, pickles and chips on plates Dee Ann suspected had been destined for paying customers.

Then she shooed the other women out front and left Dee Ann and Julian alone.

"You let her think we were a couple!" Dee Ann raged.

"But I didn't tell her we were engaged."

"Julian, this is small-town America. They're already naming our children."

"We might need the help," he said, and bit into the sandwich. "Yum. Corned beef. I wonder what wine would go with this. Obviously, German and probably white, though—"

"Beer."

"Pardon?"

"Beer. Beer and corned beef. You haven't tasted the sauerkraut yet."

"Ah." Julian explored his sandwich.

"Don't think that by changing the subject I'll forget your little boyfriend act. When Grandmother gets back here, I want you to set her straight."

Julian put his sandwich on the plate. "Your grandmother wanted to believe that we're in love and it'll make it easier to explain what's in the newspapers."

And easier to explain a possible great-grandchild. But what happened when she and Julian didn't marry? Dee Ann would look like a fool for rejecting him.

"You got on her good side by speaking German. That's low, Julian."

He shrugged. "How do you think I convinced her to sell me the property in the first place?"

Dee Ann realized she wasn't going to win the argument. After a few more days, it wouldn't matter, anyway.

She sulked until her grandmother returned.

"Did you eat, my sweet children?" Katrina sat next to Julian and propped her feet on one of the other chairs.

"Delicious." Julian complimented her.

Dee Ann scowled.

"Now, tell me why you are in the newspaper and why my phone has been ringing and ringing. And such wailing." She raised her hands and looked heavenward. "My daughter-in-law," she explained to Julian and rolled her eyes.

"Wh-what exactly did Mother say?" Dee Ann asked, dreading the response.

"Nothing that made sense. Victor tells me, though, that you have not called them, Dee Ann."

"They weren't home!"

"We did try to contact Dee Ann's parents, Mrs. Karrenbrock," inserted Julian smoothly. "This whole thing has been a huge misunderstanding."

Dee Ann noticed that he'd bypassed the word *affair*.

"But, Dee Ann, where were your clothes?"

"I had on a swimsuit. We were on a boat."

"The paper says you stole the boat."

"Reporters." Julian chuckled, interrupting Dee Ann. "We were at the Belden wedding—"

"The man who left my Dee Ann in her wedding dress with the antique lace I carried with me from the old country?" Katrina clutched her hands together before dabbing her forehead with a hankie she kept tucked in the cuff of her sleeve.

"Yes, Grandmother. We're friends now."

Katrina looked unconvinced.

"The Beldens were going to honeymoon on their yacht and I wanted to show Dee Ann the boat before they sailed," Julian said. "Unfortunately, there were roses."

"Dee Ann is allergic to roses." Katrina nodded.

Hey, he wasn't doing a half-bad job. Dee Ann sat back and let Julian continue.

"The medicine she took made her sleepy. When she fell asleep, I thought I would let her rest. Unfortunately, I fell asleep, as well, and the boat drifted without ever being anchored."

He'd skipped a lot, such as how the boat came loose

from its moorings, but Katrina accepted the paper-thin explanation.

"Well," Julian said, grimacing, "Carter thought the boat had been stolen and we didn't know where we were until we were rescued by the Coast Guard. Only, as far as they knew, we'd stolen the boat. By the time Carter and Nikki came to vouch for us, the press had been alerted."

"Such an adventure you have had, Dee Ann." Katrina clucked in sympathy.

She didn't know the half of it, which was a very good thing. "The press has staked out our house, Grandmother. And Julian's, as well, so we came here. Is that okay?"

"Yes, yes, dear one. I have wondered when you would come for the shop and this is a good time."

"Oh, but...I'm not going to take your shop. I don't want it."

Katrina raised her eyebrows. "Then why did you buy it from this man?"

"I was only acting on behalf of Carter and Nikki Belden," Julian explained. "I was never the actual owner."

"They were going to tear everything down," Dee Ann added.

"So?"

Wasn't her grandmother upset? Outraged? Didn't she feel betrayed? Didn't she understand? "But—but this has been your shop for fifty years!"

"And for fifty years I have looked forward to the day when I can retire. Louise and Brigitte are the same. We want to visit the old country again before we die. Then, in one day, Mr. Wainright makes our dream come true. He buys the coffee shop, the laundry and the drugstore all at once and with enough money for us to travel and still live comfortable lives."

"It was nothing," Julian murmured modestly. The wretch.

Katrina patted his hand. "But then, you and your papa buy it back. Why?" she asked Dee Ann.

"To save it for you."

Katrina muttered something in German. Julian raised his eyebrows.

"Anyway, I thought you'd want to buy it back now." Dee Ann had counted on it, in fact. Most of her investment capital was tied up in the purchase.

Her father had promised to reimburse her, but ever the businessman, he was still haggling with Dee Ann over the value of investments he wanted to trade for it.

It didn't help to find that Katrina had no sentimental feelings about her coffee shop.

If only Victor had listened to his daughter, they wouldn't have traded their Belden stock and would have maintained control over Belden Industries.

And Dee Ann would not now be wondering if she had been made pregnant by the Belden Industries executive vice president.

"I do not want to buy back the shop. For years, I have been talking to your father and for years he refuses to listen." Katrina threw up her hands. "Sell it to somebody else, if you want. But not me. I have spent my money on something else."

"On what?" Dee Ann had visions of smooth-talking

shysters preying on her grandmother. They looked a lot like Julian.

Katrina's eyes sparkled. "Louise, Brigitte and I are going on a world cruise!"

"A cruise? You spent your money—" *my money* "—on a world cruise?"

Her grandmother beamed and nodded.

"Does my father know about this?"

"Pfft." Katrina flapped her hands in a dismissing gesture. "I told you, he doesn't listen to me."

"That'll teach him," Julian murmured.

Dee Ann glared at him, then turned to her grandmother. "When is this cruise?" Maybe they could get a refund.

"Not until early spring, but we're going on a short cruise now to try it out. You know—" she leaned toward Julian "—to see if we get seasick or quarrel when we're traveling."

"What a wonderful idea!" Julian said.

No, it wasn't. Dee Ann tried signalling to tell him as much, but he ignored her. "When are you leaving?"

"The day after tomorrow. I told Victor to send someone to run the coffee shop, or I'd have to close it. Whatever." She slapped her knees. "It's not my problem anymore. But it's better that you're here now, Dee Ann. I can teach you a little before I go."

"But, I—"

Julian broke in. "Dee Ann and I will be delighted to run KK's in your absence."

Wasn't he listening? Her grandmother was leaving

and had no intention of running the coffee shop ever again. What was the point of keeping KK's open?

Dee Ann opened her mouth just in time to catch Julian's look of warning. All right, she'd go along with him, but he better have a fabulous explanation. Her grandmother was looking at her. "Yes, delighted," Dee Ann echoed belatedly.

"Wonderful." Katrina clapped her hands. "So we keep everything in the family, yes?"

Julian reached across the table and covered Dee Ann's hand. "Yes."

8

"THAT'S NOT the way KK's Koffee Kake batter is supposed to look," Dee Ann pronounced. She'd just put three pans of cinnamon rolls in one of the two ovens and slapped her mitts at the Velcro fasteners on the official KK's apron she was wearing. Very slick and professional, Julian thought with approval. Of course, she hadn't actually made the cinnamon rolls. Katrina had made them last night and put them in the refrigerator so they'd be ready to bake this morning. But Dee Ann *looked* as if she knew what she was doing, and in Julian's book form counted.

He eyed the foamy white stuff he was stirring in the stainless-steel vat. "That's the way the batter looked yesterday." Hadn't Katrina stirred her famous batter in this very bowl for years?

Dee Ann shook her head. "I watched my grandmother very closely and the batter did *not* bubble like that."

"Well, it's bubbling today." Julian waggled his eyebrows. "Maybe it likes us."

"Be serious." Dee Ann grabbed the recipe, which her grandmother had written from memory. "These batches are so huge, you might have made a mistake."

Or Katrina might have made a mistake. She never

bothered to measure. Just a sack of this and a shake of that, a little more flour if it looked as though it needed it, and that sort of thing. "I followed the recipe," Julian reiterated.

"I *knew* I should've made it myself!" Dee Ann poked at the batter.

Julian drew a deep breath. He was not going to argue with her. He was not going to snap at her. And he was not going to hit her on the head with a rolling pin, even though it was within reach.

Dee Ann had let him know that allowing him to make the famous coffee cake had been quite a concession on her part, but opening the shop involved a number of small chores, chores that apparently only she could do, and she was afraid the cake wouldn't be ready in time. Thus, he was granted the honor of mixing KK's Koffee Kake. He should have declined.

"You added a sack of flour and a sack of sugar?"

"Yes."

"How much milk?"

Julian pointed to the gallon jug. "Two and a half quarts."

"Nineteen eggs?"

Yes, nineteen. It was a strange number and caught his attention. "Want to count the shells?"

Dee Ann wandered over to the trash, infuriating Julian. She'd been impossible ever since he'd volunteered them to run the coffee shop. He'd explained that running KK's was the perfect excuse for them to remain in Rocky Falls. If any reporters found their way to the tiny town, Dee Ann could act as though this had been planned all along.

It was the perfect cover, and did she appreciate it? No.

This was the second morning in a row that they'd opened KK's at 5:00 a.m. The first morning, Katrina had helped them. In other words, she'd done all the cooking. This morning, she and her two friends were on their way to the Houston airport to catch a morning flight to Miami.

He and Dee Ann were on their own.

Dee Ann needed to lighten up. Running a small-town eatery could prove entertaining. Certainly different.

"Julian..." She plucked a can out of the trash. "I thought this baking powder was nearly full yesterday."

"I used it up."

Dee Ann marched over to the vat and peered in.

Julian used the big paddle to poke down the batter, which was threatening to crawl over the top.

"How much baking powder did you put in?"

"Whatever the recipe said, Dee Ann." He was becoming truly annoyed with her. He was no stranger to a kitchen and had been known to create gourmet dinners all by himself. Women usually appreciated his efforts. A lot, actually. Coffee cake, spelled with or without a K shouldn't pose much of a challenge.

"It said three-quarters of a cup."

"Look again."

"I *am*." She thrust the paper under his nose and he had to move it back to focus.

"There." He pointed. "Three cups."

"Three cups?" she shrieked.

"Dee Ann, please. Have you been drinking caffeinated tea this morning?"

"The recipe says three-*quarters*." She shook the paper at him. "You added way too much baking powder."

Perhaps he had. "I'm *sorry*. I've apparently made an error." He could have offered the excuse that Katrina's handwriting would have made a doctor proud, but didn't.

They stared at the huge stainless-steel bowl. The batter finally reached the rim and bubbled over as if auditioning for the part of foam in a beer commercial. Julian grabbed another stainless-steel bowl and started bailing batter. As soon as he filled that bowl, it was obvious that they'd need another. "It's alive, it's alive!" He thought the whole thing was amusing.

Dee Ann did not. "Faster!" she urged, wild-eyed.

"Feel free to help," Julian retorted.

She shoved a third bowl at him, then a fourth as the batter continued to grow.

"Let's dump it down the sink." Julian lifted the original vat. "We can drown it."

"No!" Dee Ann grabbed his arm, spilling batter on Julian's Italian-leather loafers. He looked down at them, then back up at her, but didn't say a word. He should get a medal.

"You used up all the baking powder."

"So buy more." She was treating this as though it were a disaster. He'd just mix another batch. Mistakes were bound to happen, though it was unfortunate that this had been his mistake.

"I *can't* until the market opens. By then it'll be too late. We'll have angry people lined up demanding coffee cake."

Afraid he'd say something he'd regret, Julian dropped the vat on the butcher block and wiped his shoes. Near his head, batter plopped onto the floor as another bowl overflowed. "Just what do you suggest we do, Dee Ann?"

They'd used up all the mixing bowls, so Dee Ann grabbed a roasting pan and poured some of the overflow into it. "We'll have to use this batter as the base for more batches. We'll just triple all the ingredients to get the baking powder ratio to come out right."

"And stir it in what?"

"The stockpot and the roasters, I guess." She looked at the crowded kitchen.

Over the café curtains at the windows, Julian looked at the pinkening sky. They should already have this batch in the oven. It needed half an hour to bake and KK's should open for early-morning customers by six-thirty. "We'd better hurry, then."

Once they added additional ingredients, the batter settled down. The problem was trying to mix the whole thing together. They couldn't. They'd need a swimming pool to hold everything.

"Julian, pour some of that in here," Dee Ann instructed. "Mine looks too dry."

Julian hefted one of the pans and dumped its contents into the stockpot. "How does that look?"

She shook her head, a worried frown pulling at her mouth. "It still doesn't look the same."

"But it'll be okay."

Dee Ann rounded on him. "Okay isn't good enough! Don't you understand? KK's Koffee Kake is famous around here. People *will* notice the difference."

Julian bit back a sarcastic reply and only said, "Then I'll let you work with the batter and I'll chop pecans for the topping. You trust me to do that right, don't you?"

"I think so," she said, seeming to seriously consider whether she could.

That was it. Time out. He was going to get another cup of coffee.

Julian pushed through the swinging doors into the customer area of the coffee shop, slipped behind the counter and poured a mug of coffee. He'd been forced to make do with an already-ground domestic coffee. That would have to change, he thought, sipping it. This was a weak and vile brew. Hardly a fitting companion for the coffee cake.

Mrs. Karrenbrock really had something with that recipe, he mused. It was simple, but very good, even to Julian's experienced tastes. With the right marketing, it could be sold as a mix.

Naturally, people would come to Rocky Falls to sample the original "kake" at the shop—which could stand updating. And the more activities tourists were offered in Rocky Falls, the more tourists would come.

The fact was, Rocky Falls had a vast untapped potential. Julian had noticed it at once when he'd visited two months ago. He'd thought that if Dee Ann and her father hadn't bought back the place from the Beldens, it might not be such a bad thing.

Julian had worked for Carter Belden for years in a position he'd created himself. He developed new projects, raised venture capital, put together deals and generally got all the fun without any of the responsibility. And that was exactly the way he wanted it.

But Belden Industries didn't develop tourist attractions and Julian found himself intrigued by the challenge.

Other central Texas towns had preserved themselves by becoming tourist areas. Rocky Falls was perfectly positioned to do the same. Actually, Julian was surprised Victor hadn't developed it long ago.

Julian would have to discuss this with Dee Ann, but there was no reason he couldn't start making a few changes now to demonstrate what a difference could be made.

Change number one: freshly ground coffee. Real milk and cream. Julian grimaced at the powdered creamer in glass shakers. Blasphemy.

Carrying his mug into the kitchen, he scooped out pecans and grabbed a knife.

Dee Ann was still fussing with the batter. Something about seeing her working in the kitchen appealed to Julian. A tortoiseshell headband kept her hair off her face and she wasn't wearing much, if any, makeup. The domestic goddess-type hadn't attracted him before and he was rather surprised, given her cranky mood and the early hour, that it was appealing to him now.

"Are you about ready for the topping?" Julian asked, mixing chopped nuts with brown sugar and cinnamon. He read the amounts with more care this time.

"No, I am *not* ready for the topping," she snapped. "The baking pans aren't greased."

"I'll do that," Julian offered. She was wound with an extra twist this morning and he could understand why. After fifty years, KK's granddaughter was running the show and no doubt the townspeople would stop by to check and compare. If he'd learned one thing about Dee Ann, it was that she didn't like to fail.

So, he'd cut her some slack. For now.

WHAT WAS THE MATTER with her? Was incompetence a virus you could catch?

Dee Ann hadn't succeeded at anything she'd tried for months. And now, something as simple as making coffee cake was beyond her.

And what about the cakes and muffins she'd have to make after the ones Katrina made yesterday were gone?

Dee Ann could cook, but not on this scale. Obviously, Julian had underestimated what it would take to keep the coffee shop open. But of course he would, she thought, sending a resentful glance his way. Men always underestimated domestic chores. Always.

Cook for an entire town? No problem.

How had her grandmother done it day in, day out, for fifty years? *For years, I have been talking to your father...* And he wouldn't listen. Typical man. Let him come up here and run the shop. He wouldn't last the day.

Dee Ann checked the batter bowls, hoping that they all contained equal ingredients. All this stirring would affect the texture of the cake, making it denser and tougher. She sighed, knowing that comparisons would be made and tongues would cluck. Customers wouldn't come back.

It didn't matter that Julian had made the actual error. Dee Ann blamed herself. Mixing KK's Koffee Kake was something that should have been done by Katrina Karrenbrock's granddaughter.

"Are the pans ready?" she called over her shoulder. Julian had been so quiet.

"Right behind you. The topping is ready, too."

"Thanks." Dee Ann started to lift the bowl.

"Here—let me get that. It's bound to be heavy." Julian hurried over.

"I can get it!" she snarled, conscious that she sounded like a shrew.

Embarrassed, she hoisted the bowl and carried it over to the butcher-block work area in the center of the kitchen.

"Watch out!" Julian shouted just as Dee Ann's foot skidded on a smear of batter.

It happened so fast. She felt her foot sliding and tried to keep her balance, knowing it was a lost cause. Batter sloshed down the front of her apron. At the last moment, she released the bowl and grabbed for the utensil racks to break her fall.

Dee Ann landed on the black-and-white-tile floor in an ocean of coffee-cake batter, more chagrined than hurt. A cold sticky wetness seeped through her white shorts.

"Dee Ann! Are you all right?" Julian squatted beside her, gazing at her with concern.

"No," she replied, staring down at herself, then up at Julian, impeccable as always. It wasn't fair.

"What's wrong? Did you break something?" He reached for her arm.

His second mistake of the morning.

Dee Ann grabbed his hand and yanked hard, hard enough to bring Julian down next to her in the batter.

He landed with a satisfying plop and she grinned. "*Now* I'm all right."

"You—" After gazing at her in astonishment, he shifted, wincing as he sat in the batter. "What an... interesting sensation. I'll have to remember this."

Dee Ann was scraping batter off her face, blouse and apron. "If you think *that's* interesting—" she scooped up a handful of batter, pulled out the neck of his shirt and dribbled it down his chest "—try this."

She had no idea what had prompted her to do that, but it seemed to fit the crazy turn her life had taken lately.

"Hmm." Lowering the bib of his apron, Julian watched the progress of the batter as it oozed down. Rubbing some between his fingers and thumb he "hmmed" again, then looked at her thoughtfully.

Dee Ann couldn't tell what he was thinking. How to enact revenge, probably.

She braced herself. She'd been really rotten to him this morning. His mistake was understandable, given the huge quantities and the scrawled, old-fashioned handwriting of her grandmother.

Dee Ann was suddenly filled with remorse. Julian was a decent, honorable man, though no pushover. He was staying with her and offering his support and she was flinging it back in his face as often as she could. He didn't have to stay in Rocky Falls. He'd probably made other plans for the two weeks Belden Industries was closed.

He was probably blazingly angry. He didn't look angry, though. His eyes alight with something she couldn't define, he offered her a slow smile.

Here it comes. He raised his arm and Dee Ann once again braced herself.

But Julian, fingers coated in the batter, reached out and traced a sticky trail along her jawline, then up over her lips, parting them.

Dee Ann automatically licked away the sweet batter, catching one of his fingers in the process.

Their eyes met.

Now she knew what he was thinking. She'd seen that look before, when they'd been on the *Honey Bee.* But that was then and this was now and a lot had happened in between.

"Julian?"

"Hmm?" He scooped more batter, dripping it down the side of her neck.

After what she'd done to him, she could hardly object, but it did tickle.

He idly traced the batter trails lower and lower until Dee Ann felt her pulse throb. She no longer felt ticklish. "Julian—this isn't turning you on or anything, is it?"

"Uh-huh." Abandoning her neck, he ran his fingers down her batter-covered legs. "Goose bumps. The batter enhances the texture of your skin."

How kind he was—it was probably razor stubble. Dee Ann tried to move her legs away, but Julian brought his other hand up and began massaging her calf, as though KK's Koffee Kake batter were some kind of exotic massage oil.

Fascinated, Dee Ann watched the slow, sensual movements of his hands. Julian had beautiful hands with long fingers.

Wearing a whimsical smile, he ducked his head and kissed her knee, his tongue licking away the batter, his eyes meeting hers.

Dee Ann swallowed. She'd had no idea that the knee was an erogenous zone.

She offered him her other knee.

Laughing lightly, he ran his tongue around her knee as if it were a giant, dripping ice-cream cone.

And she melted inside.

The batter on her thighs was drying. Julian added more, kneading the muscles, moving ever higher on her leg, watching her as he did so.

"Don't you want to do this to me?"

"I..." Where was all this leading? He didn't think...? They couldn't.... Not *here.*

Leisurely, skimming the length of her legs, Julian withdrew his hands. He thought she was too prudish to take the dare. She could see it in his eyes.

"You're wearing pants." Perhaps that wasn't the best objection she could have raised, but Julian didn't make any wisecracks.

"Unbutton my shirt."

"J-Julian."

"Do it," he whispered. Reaching around her waist, he slid her closer. At Dee Ann's soft gasp, his lips curved into a smile.

Something deep within Dee Ann responded to that smile. Without thinking about what she was doing, she pressed her hands against his shirt before working at the first button.

Her fingers were slippery. Julian guided them as she scooted the buttons through the holes. Feeling bolder, Dee Ann worked her way down to the waistband of his pants, then looked up at him.

Julian took her hand and used it to scoop up the spreading batter.

Dee Ann held it a moment, the heavy creaminess dripping through her fingers, then, giggling, smeared it across his chest.

At the first touch, she stopped laughing. The silky texture did enhance the texture of his skin. It also allowed her fingers and palms to outline the muscles of his chest.

Pushing his shirt off to his elbows, Dee Ann coated her hands and began kneading his shoulders. A sweet smell permeated the kitchen as the friction from her hands heated the batter.

"See?" Julian asked.

"This is..."

"Unbearably sensual?" he suggested.

"Kind of kinky."

"No." He took her hands and placed them on his chest.

She could feel his heart thumping.

She could feel *her* heart thumping.

Moving slowly, she traced muscles and ribs, watching as Julian's gray eyes turned molten.

A drop of batter dripped from her hair onto her cheek. Using one finger, Julian traced its path.

Dee Ann shuddered.

"Getting cold?" Julian murmured the question and rubbed her bare arms.

"No." She was hot. So hot, the batter was in danger of cooking right on her skin.

Her eyes closed, she explored every curve and hollow of Julian's torso as if she were doing it for the first time, teased by a vague familiarity with his shape.

An instant's tensing was all the warning she had before his mouth claimed hers with a sweetness only partly due to her grandmother's coffee cake batter.

Julian's kiss she remembered, and she sighed with satisfaction. But even as she recognized the similarity with his kiss in the *Honey Bee* pilothouse, she noted that this kiss was different, harder around the edges.

It was a hot kiss. A searing kiss. A we'll-continue-this-later kiss.

And she responded with a you-better-believe-it kiss before she realized what she was doing.

And when she did, Dee Ann Karrenbrock, normally cautious and shrewd, didn't care.

In fact, for good measure, she changed her kiss to a why-wait? kiss. To make sure he got the message, Dee Ann pulled toward him, levered herself to her knees and straddled his lap, pressing herself intimately against him.

He responded by burying his hands in her hair. "You are delicious..."

Dee Ann threw back her head and laughed uninhibitedly. Julian kissed her neck, nibbling at batter trails. She felt his hands untie the apron at her neck, pulling down the bib and kissing the newly exposed skin.

Then he began undoing the buttons of her blouse, having as much trouble as Dee Ann had with his shirt.

"Hurry," she whispered, rewarded by a flash in his eyes.

The air was laden with a heavy cinnamon sweetness and the sound of their breathing. After each button fell open, Julian kissed her.

Dee Ann ripped the final two.

"You're always so impatient," he murmured.

"Am I?"

"You are with me." As he spoke, he peeled her blouse off her shoulders.

She wished her bra had been a seductive lace peekaboo number. But instead, she wore a white I'm-going-to-be-on-my-feet-cooking-all-day style.

So get rid of it, prompted an inner voice, an inner voice she wanted to follow for once.

Dee Ann was in the act of reaching around her back, when a vibrating whine started and soon changed into a loud buzz.

She froze, momentarily disorientated. "The cinnamon rolls are done."

"I hear."

"The cinnamon rolls are done! What time is it?" Her watch was coated in batter.

So was Julian's, but he swiped at it until he could make out the face. "Six-fifteen."

"Great merciful heavens, we open in fifteen minutes!"

Urged by the incessant sound of the oven buzzer, Dee Ann grabbed for her blouse, which Julian had hooked on a spatula.

"Wait." He stopped her.

"Are you nuts? People will be here any minute."

"The door's locked."

"I know, we've got—"

He silenced her with a kiss so sudden and fierce, she never finished what she'd been about to say. He reached for the large mixing bowl which had landed under the work island. Dipping one finger into the small amount of batter left in it, Julian traced a line from Dee Ann's throat straight down until he ran into the edge of her bra, stopped and looked at her inquiringly.

"I can't," she whispered, knowing he couldn't hear her over the buzzer.

"Don't you want to know what it feels like?"

She stared at him, her lips parted, her breath coming quickly.

"You'll never have another chance." He leaned forward and traced the same trail with his tongue. "See? I'll clean away any stray drops." He scooped up a handful of batter and drizzled it through his fingers.

She'd gone mad, but from the moment his lips met her throat, Dee Ann's fingers were unfastening the hook at her back.

Customers would hear the buzzer and come to investigate, Dee Ann knew.

They'd call, but she wouldn't hear.

And then they'd walk around to the back and peer in the kitchen windows, looking in the sliver of space where the curtains didn't quite come together.

And they would see Katrina Karrenbrock's granddaughter throw her bra into a colander and brazenly arch her back as Julian Wainright smeared the famous Koffee Kake batter over her breasts.

They'd hear her moan louder than the oven buzzer as Julian used his tongue to thoroughly lick off every trace of the batter.

Eyebrows would raise when she pressed herself against his lean torso. Jaws would drop as she sinuously moved against him.

Fortunately for those desiring breakfast, Mr. Wainright was able to refuse the shameless invitation. With a look that could only be described as regretful, he handed the hussy a kitchen towel and rescued the cinnamon rolls just as a distinctly scorched smell became apparent.

However, it would be noted that on the first day of Katrina Karrenbrock's absence, KK's Koffee Shoppe opened late.

And the cinnamon rolls were overdone.

9

HOW WAS she supposed to make KK's famous coffee cake and not think of yesterday morning? Of the too-brown cinnamon rolls, the dash to change and shower, the mad rush of customers showing their support for Katrina's wanton granddaughter and...and Julian?

She couldn't, which was why Dee Ann had arrived at the shop an hour earlier, mixed up the day's batch of coffee cake and shoved it into the oven before he put in an appearance.

There. No coffee cake-batter massages today. She put the dirty dishes into the sink. Just before she ran water over them, Dee Ann drew a finger down the side of the mixing bowl and stared at the batter on her skin. Rubbing her thumb over her finger, she closed her eyes. Baring herself to Julian's batter-coated hands was the most outrageously erotic thing she'd ever done. If Julian hadn't called a halt, how far would she have gone?

She put her finger in her mouth and licked off the batter. Far. Really, really far.

At five o'clock, she heard a tap on the door and saw Julian, his hair still damp from his shower. It was unusual for him to appear in public that way, though most of the public was still asleep. He'd obviously rushed over here as soon as he'd discovered her absence. Dee

Ann held up her flour-coated hands. "It's unlocked," she called.

"You're here early," he commented, letting himself in the kitchen door. "Couldn't you sleep?"

After yesterday's batter interruptus? Hardly. She fussed with the cinnamon rolls, avoiding his eyes. "I wanted to get a head start so we could open on time this morning," she said, pleased with the casual efficiency in her voice. He'd never suspect she was dodging him.

Julian removed an apron from the pegs by the door and slipped it over his head. "You've got morning-after syndrome, don't you?"

She glared at him with exasperation. "That would be ridiculous, considering...everything." She gestured vaguely. "And we managed to work together all day yesterday." So why *did* she feel awkward?

"You were too busy to think. Last night, you thought." Julian began unloading the dishwasher. "I hope you thought about how you felt and whether you'd like to feel that way again."

All the air left her lungs in a whoosh. *That* was direct. Not only had she thought about how she'd felt, she'd noticed how soft her skin was now. She remembered how his hands looked as they caressed her. The expression on his face—in his eyes. The lingering scent of cinnamon and vanilla in the air. And how she had abandoned herself totally to the moment.

Who wouldn't want to feel that way again? And more?

She was wildly attracted to him and it was all wrong.

Dee Ann wanted commitment and Julian didn't.

Should she try explaining that an affair with him wouldn't be enough? That when he lost interest and moved on, she'd be devastated? That she'd be jeopardizing her chances for a husband and family?

It would be best if he just left her alone.

"You're awfully quiet." Julian walked to where she was standing and stared at the cinnamon rolls. "They didn't rise."

"No," she agreed, glad to abandon her thoughts. "Yeast is tricky. If the water I dissolved it in was too hot, it'll kill the yeast. Too cold and it won't activate it."

"Have the rolls been out of the refrigerator long?" Julian touched the corner of the pan.

"Long enough. This is as high as they're going to get." She sighed. "I can't get used to baking in these huge quantities."

"I'd cook the rolls anyway and call them cinnamon crisps." He grinned. "Special of the day."

"That's what we served yesterday," Dee Ann said, and immediately regretted bringing up yesterday. She bit her lip, hoping Julian would let it pass.

He didn't.

"Speaking of yesterday..." He tilted her chin until she faced him. "Don't worry. No pressures. No strings. Just memories."

Dee Ann knew he meant to be reassuring, but he'd confirmed what she'd been telling herself. "I know," she said. "We're each taking a different path in life. The last few days have only been where they've crossed." And recrossed.

He looked down at her, an unreadable expression in

his eyes. "I don't know, Dee Ann. Our paths are different, but we might just end up in the same place."

"IS THAT a cappuccino machine?" Dee Ann was making sandwiches for the lunch crowd when Julian, followed by Saunders, carried a huge gleaming brass contraption through the kitchen.

"Sure is," Julian said, looking pleased. "Saunders brought it with him."

"Why?"

"I asked him to."

"Why?"

Julian rolled his eyes as he backed through the door into the dining area. "Because there isn't a whole lot of taste difference between the coffee you serve here and your dishwater."

Her mouth open, Dee Ann wiped her hands and followed them into the coffee-bar area.

Julian was unplugging the four-burner coffee maker unit on the back wall. "Once Rocky Falls tastes fresh-ground, they'll never go back."

"How much did that thing cost?"

"Oh, lots." Julian peeled away plastic padding while Saunders removed pots and canisters from the bags he carried. "But I did get it used from a restaurant-supply place."

"I'll go get the coffee beans," Saunders mumbled and slid past Dee Ann without looking at her. Coward.

The late-morning patrons of KK's watched with interest as Julian set up the cappuccino machine. Dee Ann wanted to discuss the addition of an expensive, sophisticated machine in a down-home coffee shop, but Julian wisely stayed in the dining area where he knew good and well she wouldn't raise a fuss.

"Rocky Falls people just aren't the cappuccino type," was the best she could manage by way of protest.

"Not yet," Julian replied with confidence. "Anyway, what can it hurt to try?"

There was no answer to that. If Julian wanted to amuse himself with his new toy, fine. Dee Ann had sandwiches to make.

"We'll have to try this out after I get back," he said as she'd turned to go into the kitchen.

"Where are you going?"

"To Galveston with Saunders. He brought my new credit cards, but I'll have to show up in person for a new driver's license. I should be back after you close tonight."

"You mean you're leaving me here all by myself?" She'd wanted to avoid him, so why didn't she just wish him bon voyage?

He grinned as he tried to figure out where to fit all the black knobs on the machine. "You sound like you'll miss me."

"I can't work the lunch crowd all by myself!"

Picking up one of the knobs, Julian peered behind the machine. "Didn't Katrina say you could call in Brigitte's daughter?"

"Adelaide? Well, yes, but she's busy with the pies. Since Brigitte's with Grandmother, Adelaide's been getting up as early as we do."

Julian couldn't attach the knob, so he picked up another and tried it. "Tell you what. If she can't help during lunch, I'll stay, but the drivers'-license office closes at five."

He muttered something and discarded the second knob.

Dee Ann saw the instruction manual under the plastic debris. She unearthed it and handed it to him, but he waved it aside. "I'll figure this out in a minute."

Typical. Dee Ann tossed the pamphlet on the counter and went to call Adelaide. Saunders strolled back through, carrying a yardstick.

Dee Ann reached out and snagged him as she hung up the wall telephone. "The machine doesn't fit, does it?"

"It fits." He sounded defensive.

She pointed. "Then what's that for?"

Saunders looked at the yardstick in his hands as if noticing for the first time that he was holding it. "The, uh, coffee display and...stuff."

Dee Ann was about to ask about the "stuff" when Saunders grabbed her arm.

"Say! Good news, or, I should say in this case, no news is good news."

"What?"

"There wasn't anything about you or Julian on TV last night, or in the paper this morning."

Dee Ann exhaled. "What a relief."

"Yes, looks like you're yesterday's news," Saunders quipped, clearly thrilled to be able to spout clichés in context. "Did you ever talk to your parents?"

Dee Ann shook her head. "Not directly. They're in New York."

"Well, they can come back now."

Walking to the sink and scrubbing her hands, Dee Ann shrugged. "I don't think they want to."

And she knew exactly how they felt.

JULIAN STILL hadn't returned when Dee Ann walked to her grandmother's Victorian home at six.

KK's wasn't open for dinner, thank goodness. Most everyone in Rocky Falls ate at the Rocky Falls Diner or at home. If they wanted fast food, they had to drive eight miles to the interstate, where they could find a representative of just about every fast-food chain there was. Unfortunately, after all that driving, fast food wasn't truly fast.

But the last thing Dee Ann wanted to do was cook. She'd had enough of cooking, thank you. Fortunately, Katrina bought pies and other pastries from Brigitte and Adelaide. Dee Ann knew she couldn't keep the shop supplied by herself.

Still, it was grueling work and for what? Her father had paid the taxes on this property for years. KK's may have supported the Karrenbrocks once upon a time, but that time passed when the interstate bypass had been built and siphoned off the through traffic.

Julian had mentioned the potential and as Dee Ann walked past the shuttered stores, she tried to see what had caught his interest. Maybe she could use that potential as a selling point to investors if her grandmother didn't want the shop back.

Dee Ann had hoped Katrina would tire of traveling and be grateful they'd kept the shop open so she could return to the life she'd led. But after the last couple of days, Dee Ann had her doubts. What sane person would trade being pampered on a cruise ship for spending all day on her feet baking?

Dee Ann also had her doubts about whether Julian would return. She expected to get a phone call from him saying that "something had come up" and he was staying in Galveston. She also anticipated that he would check in on her until she knew whether or not she was pregnant.

If Julian stayed in Galveston, it would be for the best. She was going to have to forget about him, she told herself as she climbed the wooden porch steps. And that would be easier to do if she didn't work side by side with him every day. He simply wasn't husband material.

Dee Ann was battling the feeling of desolation that swept over her, when a white sports car zoomed down the street.

Who else could it be but Julian?

She could feel her mood lighten and, helpless to prevent the smile from spreading across her face, she knew she was doomed. How could she *ever* forget Julian Wainright?

JULIAN SQUEALED into the driveway in an adolescent display of driving. He had to do something to dispel this feeling of coming home. Home was his perfectly decorated penthouse in Galveston. Home was not a huge Victorian with dry rot.

Saunders couldn't figure out what appealed to him about this place. Julian didn't know, either, but when he saw Dee Ann standing on the porch, he began to suspect she was most of the appeal.

Stay away, he cautioned himself. He was walking a dangerous path between building a case for her to marry him if she had to and being able to walk away if she didn't.

He should have remained in Galveston where he belonged. And they definitely shouldn't be staying under the same roof. He'd seen the raised eyebrows from the townspeople, but where else was he supposed to stay? The only person in town from whom to rent rooms had college-age students living in them for the rest of the month.

No, the way to work this was to show Dee Ann the development potential of Rocky Falls. It would be perfectly natural for him to stay here a few days and work up some ideas. During that time, he'd stress their business relationship and avoid a personal one.

He sighed with regret. He now remembered every glorious instant with her on the *Honey Bee*. Talk about untapped potential. Who would ever have suspected Dee Ann Karrenbrock of being such an uninhibited lover? Certainly not Dee Ann, herself. He'd love to help her regain her memory of that night, if only to live it again.

He wouldn't mind reliving yesterday in the kitchen, for that matter. But, however difficult it would be, he was going to have to keep his distance. No fooling around until they knew whether or not she was pregnant. After that, it would be her call.

Glancing up at her as she leaned on the porch railing, Julian quickly looked away from the neckline of her shirt and strengthened his resolve.

Cutting the engine, he got out of the car. "How'd it go today?" Casual, friendly—that's the right tone.

"I survived, but I'm pooped." Demonstrating, she collapsed onto the porch swing.

"Guess what I've got?" He opened up his tiny trunk and withdrew an insulated hamper.

"A four-course dinner from Margaux's," Dee Ann guessed promptly.

When had he become so predictable? "That's right." He kept his voice light, but he was secretly annoyed at her blasé reaction.

"You're kidding!"

He shook his head.

She sat bolt upright, making him feel better. "I just picked the most unlikely thing I could think of. Oh, Julian, you're an angel!" Dee Ann ran down the steps and helped him unload the food.

His resolve crumbled. "Dee Ann?"

She turned, her arms full, and looked at him questioningly.

Right in the front yard of her grandmother's house, in full view of anyone who cared to look, Julian swooped down and kissed her full on the mouth, not releasing her until she kissed him back.

"W-what was that for?" she asked.

"A reminder." He slammed his trunk closed. "I'm no angel."

WHATEVER HE WAS, she wanted him. She'd awakened this morning and for an instant, had seriously considered creeping down the hall to his room and joining him in his bed.

Why should she keep fighting her attraction to him? She knew she was weakening and was very much afraid that she'd surrender and take him on his terms. Several times during dinner yesterday evening, she'd let her mind wander and pictured dozens of similar evenings, evenings spent sitting side by side with Julian, discussing everything under the sun. Afterward, unlike last night, they'd adjourn to the bedroom for a session of sensual delights and awaken in the morning replete and heart whole.

Could she do it? Always assuming she wasn't pregnant, could she have an affair and keep from falling happily-ever-after in love with Julian Wainright, confirmed bachelor?

Probably not. And nothing in Julian's demeanor led her to hope that his feelings for her might have grown deeper.

So, today, Dee Ann resolved to put some emotional distance between them. She had to. No more intimate dinners. Certainly no more touchy-feely fun and no more dwelling on what she couldn't have.

She was loading the dishwasher after the breakfast crowd, when Julian came sailing through, carrying a flat package in an overnight-delivery envelope.

He grabbed a butcher knife and used it to slit open the envelope, then the padded one inside. Withdrawing a box, he opened it and made a satisfied sound. "What do you think of your new menu?" he asked, handing her a folded sheet.

Dee Ann stared at a laminated, forest-green and cream menu. At the top was a stylized version of the KK's coffee-cup sign in brown. "You could have *asked* me first!"

"And what would you have said?" Julian crumpled the packaging and discarded it.

"I'd have said no."

"That's why I didn't ask first."

Dee Ann glared at him. "But Grandmother will be back in a week! What are you doing changing the menu? What if she doesn't like it?"

With an exasperated sound, Julian took the menu from her, opened it and handed it back. "I added a listing of coffees and gourmet cookies."

"We don't serve gourmet cookies."

"We do now. I found a supplier."

Dee Ann glanced at him, then scanned the menu. An assortment of coffees, teas and cookies had joined KK's regular fare.

"Coffee bars are very popular right now," Julian added. "I kept the prices lower than one would pay in the city, but you'll still have a nice profit margin. The fifty cents you charge for coffee now barely covers your cost. And people sit here and drink three or four cups. When they're drinking cappuccino, they'll be paying for each cup."

Dee Ann sighed. People had been asking about the "contraption" which had displaced the regular coffeepots several days ago. Julian hadn't been ready for it to make its debut, so Dee Ann had ignored the thing, for the most part.

"Why are you doing this?" she asked him.

He hesitated and Dee Ann suspected he'd changed his mind about what to tell her. "I see potential," he said at last. "That's the way I am. That's what I do for a living. I suppose I thought that if we fixed this place up a bit, you'd have an easier time finding a buyer."

How could she stay angry with him? He was right. "I guess I was counting on my grandmother to miss all this and come back to KK's the way she always has."

Shaking his head, Julian finished loading the dishwasher. "If you'd seen her glee when she sold KK's a couple of months ago, you wouldn't think that. She was so thrilled to unload this place, if I hadn't been in such a hurry, I wouldn't have had to pay so much for it."

He was casually speaking of the time when he and the Beldens had outmaneuvered her. Maybe she could tap into some residual anger there. No. That was in the past and she'd come to terms with it. "But Grandmother hadn't been away from the shop, then."

"I think that was the whole idea."

Shrugging, Dee Ann stared down at the menu. It looked great and wasn't so ambitious that she couldn't handle the additions, either. Slowly, she gathered the old battered menus that nobody asked for, anyway. "The only thing is that this color scheme clashes with the blue and yellow."

"Ah." Julian held up a finger. "I was just coming to that."

"What have you done?" she asked instantly.

"I took the liberty—"

"You've been taking lots of liberties, lately."

"Not as many as I'd like." Julian gave her a dry smile and Dee Ann fell silent. "When I was at the restaurant-supply house, I found a group of chairs and tables they'd bought from a pizza place that had gone out of business." He tapped the menu. "They're natural wood upholstered in this green color. The tables have a matching green inlaid in the center. I picked out the best ones and bought them."

Dee Ann gasped. "Just like that?"

Julian nodded. "Pretty much."

"This place can't afford new furniture. I swear, I'm not sure we've broken even a single day this week."

"I know we haven't." He picked up one of the old menus. "These prices haven't changed in twenty-five years. But when I ran to the store for baking powder, I sure paid the going rate. No wonder the place is crowded in the mornings. People can eat here cheaper than they can eat at their own homes."

"That's not true." But her protest lacked conviction.

"Close enough." He tossed the old menu into the trash, then added the others to it. "I'll warn you that I did adjust the prices, but not as much as they should be."

"You raised the prices without telling me?" Dee Ann grabbed the new menu. She'd been so concerned with the coffee-bar items, she hadn't even looked at the rest.

"You should have consulted with me." She met his eyes. "This wasn't your decision to make."

"I wanted it to be a surprise," he began, with a smile meant to charm her.

"Don't patronize me."

Her icy tone froze the smile right off his face. "All right. Consider it an experiment. I wanted to see if I could make this place pay for itself. You've been so hardheaded—"

"What!"

"You know, the 'we must follow the coffee-cake recipe exactly because it is a sacred trust' routine," he said in a deep voice.

"Since I am the owner, that would be my prerogative."

"And since you're the owner, you'll know a great deal when you hear one," Julian retorted. "This is my experiment, I'll pay."

"This isn't about money. It's about you making decisions without consulting me."

"Acknowledged." Julian dug in the trash for the old menus. "If you'll allow me to experiment, I'll save the old furniture and curtains—"

"Curtains?"

"I called my decorator. Don't worry about it." He dismissed the fee of a professional decorator as if it were nothing. "I'll tell you what. If you don't like the changes, I'll take everything with me when I leave."

Dee Ann was in her businesswoman mode. Quickly thinking over his proposition, she found nothing against it. "That's fair. I agree." She held out her hand

and Julian shook it as though they'd just negotiated a business deal. Which was exactly what they'd done.

He held on to her hand. "I did want to paint the walls a café au lait color, but I suppose that's out of the question?"

Dee Ann looked at the pale yellow walls, speckled with years of stains. She hated yellow. "Did you order paint?"

Julian nodded. "Since tomorrow is Sunday, I figured we could close early today, work all day tomorrow and reopen Monday with a new look."

Dee Ann considered it and was tempted. Very tempted. The room wasn't that large, and with the two of them working, it wouldn't take long to paint. What a kick to see if they could rejuvenate this small corner of Rocky Falls, not to mention the increase in its value when the time came to put KK's on the market.

Julian was silent, letting her think. At last, she nodded and smiled. "Okay, it's a deal."

10

JULIAN STARED at the display of pregnancy-test kits, then checked his watch. He'd slipped next door to Main Street Drugs right before closing, thinking he'd grab one of these handy-dandy kits for Dee Ann. It had been a week since his night with her aboard the *Honey Bee*. A week in which his past life had flashed before his eyes. A week in which he had become acquainted with facets of Dee Ann Karrenbrock he'd never suspected were there.

Except for his friendship and working relationship with the Beldens and Saunders, Julian knew more about Dee Ann than he knew about anyone else. And the more he learned about her, the more he realized how much he didn't know about the people he considered his closest friends.

For instance, he knew nothing about Carter's and Nikki's families, except for those he'd met at the wedding. And as for Saunders, he had no idea what Saunders did outside of work. Naturally, they all spent most of their waking moments working or socializing—during which, they discussed work.

Julian had thought he was living a rich and varied life.

He wasn't. He was living a rich and two-dimensional life.

Julian had also thought he was perfectly content with those two dimensions.

And he was, until...until now, he'd thought, but upon reflection, he realized he'd felt unsettled since Dee Ann had left that long-ago party with Carter.

Had she taken something with her, or just pointed out something that had been missing? And what was that something?

For a moment, he imagined living the kind of life Dee Ann wanted. He envisioned his penthouse, the perfect groupings of designer furniture pushed aside to accommodate a playpen, bright primary-colored plastic toys scattered across the white carpet and a high chair pulled up to the Daniel Stratten dining ensemble.

No. The horrible vision cleared and he was once again facing the meager display of pregnancy-test kits in Main Street Drugs.

Wiping a hand across his temple, Julian grabbed one of the boxes on the shelf in front of him. How long did a woman have to wait to take these tests, anyway?

Dee Ann had refused to discuss anything about her possible pregnancy with him and Julian found the waiting nearly unbearable. It was time for a nudge—a thoughtful hint. His entire future was on hold until she took this test and the inactivity frustrated him.

Naturally, the waiting must be a hundred times worse for Dee Ann. He'd clearly stated his intention to support her, but she wouldn't discuss marriage unless it became necessary. So wasn't it time to find out just where things stood?

He could feel the eyes of the pharmacist on him and he looked up.

"May I help you, sir?" the man asked. He was slightly younger than Julian and had grown a mustache, probably to inspire confidence in the older population of Rocky Falls.

"Well..." Julian gestured to the kits. "Which of these works the fastest?"

"They only take a few minutes." The pharmacist came out from behind the drug counter, carefully locking the door behind him. He reached for one of the kits, flipped it over and sighed. "Expired. I was afraid of that. We don't sell many of these."

"I guess the population isn't booming around here, is it?" Just as he'd thought, Rocky Falls was crying out for rejuvenation.

Shaking his head, the pharmacist pawed through the remaining kits, discarding all of one brand. "People our age have to leave to find jobs. Here, try this one." He handed Julian a different box.

"Thanks." Julian followed him to the cash register, noting that it was an old-fashioned one where the numbers had to be punched in. "Great piece. Beautiful brass work."

The pharmacist smiled. "Just for show. I've got a computer in the back." The drawer popped open. "This is the same register my grandfather used when he opened this place."

After expressing his appreciation to the pharmacist

for staying open late, Julian walked past a dark KK's and down Main Street.

As he passed store after store, Julian visualized a revitalized Rocky Falls. With a steady influx of tourists and a bed-and-breakfast draw of some sort, the population would grow, or at least stabilize.

The area was beautiful, set amid gently rolling hills, and close enough to the major urban centers of Texas to partake of their advantages without suffering the disadvantages of crime, traffic and pollution.

All in all, it could be a great place to raise a family.

And maybe by tomorrow morning, he'd know whether or not he was going to.

A KNOCK ON HER DOOR woke Dee Ann from a sound sleep. Squinting at the clock on her bedside table, she fell back against the pillows and groaned. "Julian?" It couldn't be Julian. He wouldn't be so cruel.

The door swung open and Julian backed his way in.

"Why did you wake me up?" Dee Ann complained. "This is my *one* morning to sleep in."

"I brought you breakfast in bed." Julian was already dressed and looking his usual fabulous self.

It was too early for fabulous. Dee Ann slid one of her pillows over her head. "Go away. I'm not hungry."

There was silence.

Cautiously, she peeked out from under her pillow. Julian looked down at her, an uncertain expression on his face. "Are you, ah, feeling...unwell?"

"I'm feeling sleepy."

"More tired than usual?"

Dee Ann pushed the pillow away from her face and sat up. "Of course! I've been getting up and working on my feet all day long this entire week. Aren't *you* more tired than usual?"

"Somewhat. Which is why I brought you breakfast in bed."

She should be grateful but all she was doing was snapping at him. She always snapped at him, though, didn't she? Vowing to be more pleasant, difficult though it would be, she arranged the covers and settled herself.

And then she saw the bed tray.

Julian lowered it and stood back, obviously waiting for her reaction.

"Oh, that's lovely, Julian. A single carnation, whole-wheat toast, tea—"

"Decaf," he told her.

"—bananas and strawberries...and a home pregnancy test kit." She forced a smile. "Very elegant."

"And you'll notice the pink carnation matches the box."

"So it does." She ignored the box and sipped her tea, hoping he'd go away.

Julian still stood by her bed. "I know the, uh, waiting has been as difficult for you as it has been for me." He caught himself. "I meant, of course, that it's been far more difficult for you than it has been for me." He winced. "Not to imply that, because it hasn't been as difficult for me, I'm not concerned. Merely that as a man, I couldn't possibly—"

"Julian?" Dee Ann stopped him before he could make the awkward situation worse. "It's okay."

"Good." Hands shoved in his pockets, he stared at the tray—and then proceeded to make the awkward situation worse. "So, I thought that the least I could do was to relieve you of this tiny chore. Not that I considered it a *chore*," he added quickly. "It was my pleasure."

"Pleasure?" Dee Ann glanced from the box to him.

"Not *pleasure*. This isn't a pleasant situation and it's one *I've* never been in before—and I don't mean to imply that you *have* been in it before—"

"Julian!" She cut him off, hardly recognizing this nervous man as the suave Julian Wainright. "You're babbling."

He exhaled in a whoosh. "And, thank God, you've stopped me."

The silence that followed was almost worse than Julian's chatter.

Dee Ann choked down a strawberry, very much afraid she was turning the same shade of red.

"Shall I hold the tray while you get out of bed?" he finally asked.

"I haven't finished my breakfast yet," she mumbled. What did he plan to do, follow her into the bathroom?

He forced a smile. "By all means, finish your toast before it grows cold."

She intended to—by taking tiny little bites. "I don't see the morning paper on the tray." *Go away, go away.*

"If you want something to read...perhaps the directions to this?" In an elaborately casual gesture, Julian picked up the kit and offered it to her.

Her face hot, Dee Ann plucked the box from his fingers and tossed it at the foot of the bed. "It's too early to take a pregnancy test."

"But the pharmacist said it would only take a few minutes."

"But not *today*. I should wait at least until the end of the week," she said before a horrible thought occurred to her. "What pharmacist?" She gripped her toast with suddenly cold fingers.

"The guy at the drugstore next to KK's."

"You bought a home pregnancy kit from Tony, Jr?" she wailed.

"Youngish-looking guy with a mustache?" Julian asked.

"Oh, no. You didn't." She closed her eyes, imagining the scene. Imagining what Tony must have thought.

"Yes, I did." Julian picked up the test and positioned it carefully on her dresser. "He's been in the coffee shop a couple of times and I was returning the business."

She was never going to leave this bed. No, she was going to leave the bed in the dead of night and slink away to a convent. Or the Foreign Legion, if the nuns rejected her for having loose morals.

"What's the matter?"

"What's the *matter?*" Dee Ann moaned. "Have you lost your mind?"

"I don't understand."

"Gee, Julian, why not just post an announcement in KK's window for the entire town to see?" She gestured with her hands. "'Dee Ann Karrenbrock might be pregnant. Watch this space for details.'"

"Calm down. The man is a professional, Dee Ann."

"I'm sure he is, but he's also Adelaide's *son*." She practically spit out the word. "Tony and I used to play together when I visited Grandmother. We even dated a couple of times." She groaned again and covered her face with her hands. "This is going to be all over town by the time church is out."

Julian sighed heavily, the way a man sighs when he's confronted with an irrational woman he hopes to calm down. "Surely people have more interesting topics of discussion."

"Julian, this is a small town. And when an unmarried man buys a pregnancy kit, that *is* an interesting topic of discussion."

"So I bought a home-test kit." He shrugged. "They don't know it's for you."

"They certainly know it's not for you!"

"Okay, then they don't know it's for *us*." He pointed back and forth between them.

"And just what do you mean by that?" she asked, each word distinct.

Julian, in a rare lapse of judgment, explained. "I might not necessarily be the father." He caught the look on her face and hastily added, "Or you might not be the mother."

"Who *else?*" Dee Ann threw up her arms, sloshing her tea. "I come to town in a blaze of tawdry publicity, then shack up with you at my grandmother's. People in Rocky Falls aren't stupid or naive. They've got cable."

Julian hid a smile, which infuriated Dee Ann. "How could you do this to me?"

"Because I had no idea my pharmaceutical purchases would be the subject of town gossip!" he snapped.

"Purchases?" She keyed on the word. "What else did you buy there? Condoms?" Her voice squeaked.

"Would that have been better? Shall I stock up right now?"

"No!" She clutched his arm. "Promise me you won't buy condoms in Rocky Falls!"

He gave her a heavy-lidded look. "Are you suggesting that I buy them elsewhere, my darling?"

"I'm not suggesting you buy them at all!"

He heaved a regretful sigh. "I thought not."

"No, wait." Dee Ann held out her hand. "Maybe you should," she said seriously. "Yes! After a couple of days, go buy condoms. That way, no one will think I'm pregnant."

Julian burst into laughter. "But what if you are?"

Yes, there was that. Dee Ann felt trapped. How could this be happening to her? She felt as though she were living somebody else's life.

The bed shifted as Julian sat next to her. Taking her hand, he apologized. "I'm sorry that I've caused you further stress. We...could let it slip that we eloped, should it become prudent."

"That's lying," she said dully.

"Is it?"

"Well, isn't it?"

"Not necessarily." He shifted on the bed. "Think about it. We had a wedding. We had witnesses."

"It was a joke."

"But Roy Peabody is a judge."

"Who's Roy Peabody?"

"He was a guest at the wedding and he signed the license."

"You're kidding."

"Regretfully, no." Julian shook his head.

"I'm going to be sick." Dee Ann tried to get out from under her tray, but Julian wouldn't budge.

"Wait. If you'll recall, there's no legal record of our wedding. Anyway, we don't even know if the license was still valid."

"And we'll never know, because I tore it up." Dee Ann couldn't decide whether she was glad or not.

"We'd have to file another license, but only we would have to know," he suggested. "Or we could throw a huge bash and call it a renewal of our vows."

She eyed Julian thoughtfully. "Saunders wouldn't like for you to talk to me like this, you know."

"I know."

"With a good lawyer, a woman in my position could make things difficult for you."

"So sue me." He smiled and Dee Ann felt her heart turn over.

"Saunders would love that, wouldn't he?"

"Actually, he probably would, but I wouldn't use Saunders. I'd throw myself on your mercy." He picked up the carnation and brushed it across her lips.

What a rogue. He was finessing her and she didn't even mind. "I'm sorry I snapped at you."

"You were entitled."

"No." She gave in to impulse and drew her hand across his cheek. "You've been wonderful through this whole thing."

He turned his head and kissed her palm, sending tingles up her arm. *If only he loved me.* As the thought whispered through her mind, his eyes met hers.

Dee Ann's heart accelerated. *Does he know what I'm thinking?* She had a feeling her thoughts were on her face for him to read. He certainly stared at her long enough, long enough for wariness to creep into his eyes.

She slowly withdrew her hand.

She was falling in love with him and fighting it every step of the way. This wasn't the man to give her heart to. He didn't want it.

But she wished he did. Their situation would be so very much simpler if Julian loved her. Then she could love him back.

Julian looked away first. "If we're going to get all the painting done today, we'll have to start soon." He stood carefully, to avoid jostling her tea. "I'll walk over to KK's and start setting up."

He smiled briefly, impersonally, and was gone.

He didn't love her. She knew it as plainly as if he'd spoken. Because if he loved her, he'd want to marry her without knowing the results of the stupid pregnancy test.

Not only that, he didn't *want* to love her. She saw it in his eyes. Julian Wainright wanted no emotional entanglements.

As his footsteps echoed down the stairs, Dee Ann felt tears well up in her eyes. Across the room, the home pregnancy kit mocked her. It held the answer to her future, but it would be a future without Julian unless something drastically changed his feelings toward her in the next few days.

WHEN SHE ARRIVED at KK's, Julian had already shoved all the tables and chairs to the center of the room and draped them in sheets of plastic.

"Are we ready to paint?" She should have hurried more than she had, but she'd needed time to collect herself before facing him again.

"As soon as I take down the curtains and rods."

He jumped down from a chair and walked over to the coffee bar. "Here. This will protect your clothes." Julian tossed her an oversize T-shirt identical to the one he was wearing.

"Belden Industries 10K Run?" Dee Ann slipped it on over her clothes. "I didn't know you were a runner." Though he had the long, lean body of a runner.

"I ran for a few months, but I don't anymore. Carter sponsored a charity run during our fitness craze a few years ago."

"Why did you stop?"

"Because Carter turned it into a contest. If I ran five miles, he'd run six and so on." Julian pried the lid off a can of paint. "Why don't you stir this while I finish taking down the curtains?"

Dee Ann nodded and dipped the paintstick into the can.

Friendly, but impersonal. Keep to neutral subjects. Remain faultlessly polite. Those were the new operating rules. Julian might as well have posted them on the wall, they were so plain.

As soon as he'd suspected her feelings were becoming deeper, he'd withdrawn. Instantly. Completely.

He'd probably done it countless times before, she realized. This was a man who wouldn't commit, yet he would propose to her if she was pregnant and that rankled.

What would it take to break through Julian's defenses?

What would it take to make him fall in love with her?

Could she make him fall in love with her? Dee Ann stirred the paint and thought. She had five days before she'd take the test, since she wanted to know one way or the other before her grandmother returned.

Five days. She smiled. She'd done more with less.

For the rest of the day, she was so agreeable, her teeth hurt. She complimented Julian on his faultless taste, worked like a fiend and was even polite to Gloria, the decorator from Galveston.

The restaurant-supply company delivered Julian's new furniture and carted off the old cracked-vinyl pieces. Dee Ann didn't complain about the extra cost for a Sunday delivery. No, she smiled and complimented Julian on his good bargaining skills.

Up went the curtains, dark green fabric on gleaming brass rods. Dee Ann helped Gloria haul in large plants in brass planters from her van, then took a break. Julian kept working, arranging the furniture and adding finishing touches.

Dee Ann complimented him on his attention to detail.

However, at the end of day one, she was forced to admit that flattery had gotten her nowhere.

Day two, Monday, dawned with the grand opening of the "new" KK's Koffee Shoppe. Word quickly spread and they were inundated with customers. All commented on the new color scheme as if Dee Ann were unaware of the changes.

The coffee bar was a hit, to her surprise. There were a few grumbles about the price increases, which she expected, but all in all, Julian's redo looked as though it was a success.

Dee Ann acknowledged his superior business acumen and suggested they celebrate with a lovely champagne.

Julian demurred, pointing out that possibly-pregnant women should avoid alcohol consumption and that he would join her in abstinence. Besides, she needed her sleep and he had paperwork to do.

And then he proceeded to do it.

"If you could change this town, develop it any way you wanted, what would you do?" Dee Ann asked during the midmorning lull on Tuesday, day three. She'd listen and give her input, demonstrating how supportive she could be and how two heads were better than one.

"Come on and I'll show you," Julian replied, his face lighting up.

Good move, she congratulated herself.

He flipped the hanging sign to Closed and drew her out the door.

"We've still got on our aprons," Dee Ann protested.

"We're not going far." He smiled at her, and Dee Ann sighed, thinking she'd follow him anywhere—if he only asked.

Julian walked past the drugstore, to the end of the block, and stopped across from an old free-standing building, which had been empty for as long as Dee Ann could remember.

"Look." He pointed up and down the street. "Now, imagine new storefronts in a fifties vein."

"Julian, they look straight out of the fifties now!"

"Think restoration. New street lamps. The drugstore the way it used to be then. Penny candy. A soda fountain. Tony even has this wonderful period cash register."

She tried to think fifties, instead of how Julian discovered the period cash register in the drugstore.

"Now, over here—" he gestured across the street "—these buildings would be remodeled into shops selling local crafts—"

"Oh, come on. Crafts are so overdone."

"Okay, maybe not crafts, but specialty shops of some sort." He pointed again. "Tear down that building and turn the land into a parking lot."

She needed to pay attention and nodded to convince him that she was. "Yes, I agree that building needs to go. And that's the perfect place for a downtown lot. We could turn the land next to it into a park with a gazebo." She was getting caught up in his enthusiasm.

"Right. Because once that building's gone, you'll have an unobstructed view of the falls."

"Such as they are."

"I realize they're modest, but Dee Ann, where's your vision?"

On you.

"The falls could be a real drawing card. I've been scouting the area and I think it would be a tremendous place for a country theater and restaurant."

"In other words, a dinner theater."

He shook his head. "Yes, but we won't call it that because it has dreadful connotations of canned corn, overdone meat and has-been actors. No, I'm thinking of a continental restaurant, a superb wine cellar and an attached theater-in-the-round. Only classy events would be held there."

"You're really getting into this." Dee Ann was surprised. Stunned, actually. She was also beginning to have a few ideas of her own. "Naturally, after such a lovely evening, no one will want to drive home."

"Exactly." Julian beamed. "Your grandmother's house, which I believe you own, will make a perfect bed and breakfast. It's got six bedrooms."

"Yes," Dee Ann said slowly, beginning to see the possibilities for converting the house into an elegant bed and breakfast.

On Wednesday, day four, she discussed those possibilities again with Julian. She'd wanted to show him that they had compatible decorating tastes. She could make his life comfortable; that was her theme for the day and she concentrated on it as they walked from room to room.

Julian's enthusiasm was contagious and his approval made her hopeful. There were so many times when he said "we" in speaking of the future. So many times when he touched her arm or took her hand.

And yet, at the end of the day, Julian sat in the parlor and worked on his plans for the town instead of romancing Dee Ann.

On day five, her last chance, Dee Ann decided to bring out the heavy artillery.

Julian was physically attracted to her, this she knew. Okay, she'd work with that. It was *certainly* not a great sacrifice on her part.

"It's so hot in here," she said, fanning herself with her hand. The kitchen was hot because she'd deliberately kept the ovens going all day and this was August. And she'd temporarily thrown the air-conditioning fuse. She slipped off her apron, revealing her shortest shorts. Making sure Julian was in the vicinity, she tugged her shirttail out and tied it in front of her in a midriff-revealing style, then stretched her arms over her head.

Next, feeling like a 1940s pinup girl, she bent over to check the brownies she'd added to the coffee-bar menu. The ones from Julian's supplier had nuts in them and some people didn't like nuts, was her excuse.

Julian missed—or ignored—her performance, so Dee Ann dropped a spatula on the floor. "Oops!" she chirped.

When he turned to see what she'd dropped, Dee Ann bent over, allowing her shirt to fall forward. When she raised her head to give him a sultry look, she found that she was alone.

On yet another pan of brownies, she "burnt" her finger.

"Ow." She pouted and stuck her finger in her mouth.

"Need help?" ask a harassed-looking Julian, his arms filled with plates of sandwiches, pickles and chips.

Dee Ann slowly pulled her finger from her mouth. "Kiss it and make it better?"

Julian blinked, stared at the plates, then set them down. Reaching for her wrist, he dunked her hand under cold running water.

And so it went until that evening when a towel-wrapped Dee Ann stood wet and shivering in the upstairs hallway so she could intercept Julian. At last, she heard his footsteps on the stairs and stepped forward.

"Oh!" She gasped softly and pretended to tighten her towel.

He swallowed. "Excuse me. I thought you'd retired for the evening."

He sounded stuffy, which was the way Julian sounded when he was feeling pressured. Good.

Dee Ann laughed with a low throaty chuckle and let her towel slip. She'd been practicing. "Don't be ridiculous. I ran out of soap and was checking your bathroom for another bar." She held it up, even though there *hadn't* been extra soap in Julian's bathroom.

Wordlessly, he stood aside to let her pass.

Dee Ann sauntered forward. "I was taking a bubble bath," she informed him as she drew alongside. "Do men ever take bubble baths?"

"I can't speak for all men."

"Do *you* take bubble baths?"

"No."

"But the bubbles feel *so* good." Dee Ann accompanied this with a little shimmy.

Julian's chest rose and fell.

"Don't you wonder what all that tickling feels like?"

"No." His voice was hoarse.

Dee Ann shrugged and Julian's gaze fell. Oh, goody. Her towel had slipped a little more. "Well, *I* think you're missing out." As she turned, she dropped the soap, which bounced and skidded across the wooden floor.

Dee Ann hadn't counted on the soap moving. She'd wanted to bend over and tease Julian, but this worked out great. They both reached for the soap at the same time and collided.

Dee Ann clutched Julian to break her fall and in so doing felt her towel drop between them.

They froze.

While she hadn't intended to go quite this far, what's done was done. And very nicely, too.

"I'm so sorry," he apologized in a rough whisper, his hands warm on her arms.

"I'm not."

He didn't move. She *wanted* him to move, damn it! She was standing against him, naked from the waist up. All he had to do was step back and the towel would fall to her feet.

Why didn't he?

His face was a mask and she was losing her nerve.

Then she felt his hands at her waist and smiled, swaying toward him—until she realized he was trying to cover her up.

No! She still clutched his shirt and with a deep, primal roar, she ripped it apart.

The both gasped as buttons skittered across the floor.

Dee Ann's towel fell, but she didn't notice, because Julian, his eyes wide and his jaw set, backed away, turned on his heel and left her standing in the hallway.

She heard his footsteps continue down the stairs, across the foyer and out the front, banging the screen door behind him.

Moments later, she heard the engine of his car start, then grow faint as he drove out of her life.

11

LOUIE'S MOTEL—Truckers Welcome.

An excellent spot to take stock of his situation, Julian thought as he sat by the window in the darkened room. He'd left the curtains open so the flashing Truckers Welcome sign periodically bathed the room in a rosy glow.

If only life were as rosy. Obviously, Dee Ann was pregnant and in the grip of procreating hormones. Nature's logic escaped him. What was the point of turning up a pregnant woman's lust level? And Dee Ann's was set to the boiling point. She obviously wasn't herself. Not that he didn't appreciate this particular facet of her personality.

He'd noticed the change in just the past few days. That's when the hormones must have kicked in. Dee Ann had hung on his every word as though he were an oracle from on high, and then yesterday, she'd *nested*. That was the only way to describe all her plans for the house. Oh, she'd said she was thinking of the bed and breakfast, but Julian wasn't fooled. This was a woman who was nesting.

And then today...he fingered the edges of his buttonless shirt. She'd become a wild woman.

At any other time—*any* other time, he would have

been delighted. Thrilled. Encouraging, even. But he'd taken advantage of her once, or twice, if he counted fooling around in the cake batter, and he wasn't going to do so again.

So. He was going to become a family man. Julian mentally waved goodbye to his former life-style and vowed that Dee Ann would never know that he was anything other than happy with his lot in life.

And there were distinct advantages. There would be more nights like the night on the *Honey Bee*, especially if the scene in the hallway was any indication.

He smiled, feeling a measure of contentment. This marriage business wasn't going to be bad at all.

ON THE MORNING of day six, a swollen-eyed Dee Ann took her pregnancy test.

Julian hadn't come back last night. His bed hadn't been slept in and his car was gone.

Obviously, her five-day campaign had backfired. He had lost whatever fleeting interest he'd had for her and, if not for her possible pregnancy, would have moved on as he'd moved on before.

He no longer found her attractive. He no longer wanted her. He certainly didn't love her.

But she loved him. She knew that now. She'd been half in love with him when she'd left him for Carter. She'd known she was going to get hurt, had tried to prevent it, but in the end, she'd fallen in love, deeply, desperately in love with Julian Wainright, the poster man for bachelors.

But when—if—he proposed, she'd turn him down.

Dee Ann set the plastic test wand on her night table, then lay back on the bed and stared at the ceiling. How ironic. She'd been willing to marry Carter without love, but she wasn't willing to marry Julian with love.

She had everything in common with Carter and they would have built a strong marriage on a solid foundation because they had similar goals. That was the key to a successful partnership. Love had nothing to do with it.

She and Julian had extremely different goals, but an intense physical attraction to each other. Or at least until last night, they had.

What had gone wrong? Dee Ann closed her eyes as she unwillingly relived the humiliation. She'd flung herself at him. And he'd clearly rejected her. There was no way to misinterpret his actions. No, when you stand naked before a man, rip off his shirt and he walks away, he's sending a pretty clear signal.

She never wanted to see him again. Ever.

Dee Ann folded her hands over her still-flat stomach. How many times had she imagined carrying a child? She'd never expected to feel maternal yearnings as strong as she did. They'd driven her to leave her father's company and devote the past three years to finding a life partner.

She'd botched the job with astonishing thoroughness.

Well, it was time to find out just how bad it was. Time to find out whether Julian would be out of her life completely, or whether she'd have to endure bittersweet contact with him for years.

Taking a deep, calming breath, Dee Ann slowly

turned her head to the nightstand and stared at the test results.

And then she burst into tears.

JULIAN HEARD her crying as soon as he walked in the front door.

That was it, then. She was pregnant. He gripped the polished wooden railing and stared into the middle distance for a moment, then squared his shoulders and climbed the stairs.

When he reached the door of her room, he saw Dee Ann curled into a ball on her bed, her hands clutched into fists, her face buried in the pillow.

He'd seen many sides of her, the fierce business competitor, the society woman, the cook and the jailbird. He'd seen her in her childhood room and he'd shared a bed with her. He'd seen her happy, triumphant, horrified, aroused and furious. He'd seen her embarrassed and humiliated.

But he'd never seen her in despair. And knowing he was the cause of it made him want to beat his fists against his chest in primal penance.

He was appalled at his incredible selfishness. All he'd thought about was how this would affect *his* life and *his* freedom. Since she'd wanted children, he hadn't considered that she might be upset about the pregnancy. Now he realized that while Dee Ann wanted children, she obviously didn't want *his* children.

He, Julian Wainright, was a cad.

Dee Ann Karrenbrock was an incredible woman and he was lucky she was going to be his wife. They would have a rich, fulfilling life together. With children. Plural. Just the way she wanted. And he was going to tell her so.

"Dee Ann." As he approached the bed, he spoke quietly to avoid startling her, but she apparently didn't hear him.

"Dee Ann?" He reached for her shoulder.

She jerked it away. "Get out!"

"No. Dee Ann," he began, easing himself onto a corner of the mattress. "We—"

He broke off as she scuttled to the far edge of the bed. *She* was rejecting *him*, the father of her child.

Julian had not anticipated this. He'd always told her they'd get married if she was pregnant, and he'd never considered that she wouldn't be in complete agreement.

He couldn't let her go through this by herself. Stretching across the bed toward her, he tried to gather her in his arms.

"Leave me alone!"

"Not like this." Moving next to her, he put his arms around her as she struggled to get away. "Shh. It's okay. I want to be here with you."

"Well, save your pity. I don't need it!"

Profoundly affected by her actions, Julian held on tightly until she gave up her struggle and sobbed quietly.

He felt like joining her, but instead held her close, spoon-fashion. "Everything will be all right," he promised, stroking her hair. He'd make it so.

"You d-don't understand." She hiccuped on a sob.

Yes, he did. "I want us to get married. Right away."

This set her off again. Julian didn't have to see her face to know she wasn't crying tears of joy. "We'll have a small, but elegant wedding—" Dee Ann cried harder. "Okay, we'll have a huge production and the finger-counters be damned."

"No." She shook her head. "You don't want me."

He sighed against her back. "You're talking about last night, aren't you?"

She nodded. Ah, progress.

"I left *because* I wanted you. I didn't want to take advantage of you."

"Why stop now?"

He was glad she couldn't see the self-disgust on his face. "I'm not stopping now. I'm going to badger you until you agree to marry me."

Dee Ann reached for a box of tissues and blew her nose, then she settled back against him. She fit nicely, Julian noted, liking the feel of her against him. Her hair tickled his chest, which was exposed by the torn shirt he still wore. He bent his legs until they touched hers.

"It wouldn't work."

Julian had lost the train of the conversation for a moment, then realized she was talking about marrying him. "We'll make it work."

"You don't want to be married, do you, Julian?"

That was a trick question. "I didn't, but I do now." He hoped he sounded sincere. He *was* sincere. He'd never ruled out marriage completely, just postponed it indefinitely.

"Oh, no." She shook her head, making him smile at

the feel of her hair brushing his throat. "You only proposed because—"

"Shh." They both knew why he'd proposed and it wasn't flattering to Dee Ann. "I'll admit that I was doing the right thing, but for the wrong reasons."

Dee Ann had gone very still. Encouraged that he'd taken the right tack, Julian continued. "I've been thinking a lot since we've come to Rocky Falls. Obviously, I was ready to consider marriage since I agreed to the ceremony, or whatever, on the beach."

"You were drunk."

Not all that drunk, but he wasn't going to argue about it. "Then my subconscious agreed to the ceremony, so plainly, my subconscious was ready to get married."

"And then your subconscious seduced my subconscious."

He smiled. "Yeah, they really like each other. So who are we to stand in their way?"

She chuckled softly and he pressed his advantage. "You know, since Carter and Nikki got back together, the dynamics have been different at Belden. I'm beginning to feel like a fifth wheel."

"Have you told them how you feel?" she asked. "I know they wouldn't exclude you on purpose."

"I don't think so, either...but it might be time for me to move on. There's an area that's intrigued me, but not one Carter ever had any interest in."

"What area?"

Julian hesitated, finding that her opinion mattered to

him. "A restaurant. I've always wanted to own my own restaurant."

"What a coincidence." She sniffed. "I've got one for sale, cheap."

He laughed. "No, I want to build one from the ground up. You know that piece of land that I said would make a good park?"

"Overlooking the falls?"

He nodded, seeing the building in his mind's eye. "That's where I want to build it."

There was silence, then, "Your dinner theater?"

"Please." He shuddered and she chuckled. "I want a continental restaurant with a first-class chef. The *separate* theater would be for intimate performing groups and plays. Lectures, perhaps. I'd enjoy booking them, as well."

"But your restaurant will be out in the middle of nowhere."

"That's the point. I want this whole area to become a trendy weekend-getaway spot. And I want to develop it with you."

"You do?"

The disbelief in her voice irritated him. "Isn't that what I've been saying?"

At first, Julian thought she was struggling again, but Dee Ann was just turning in his arms to face him.

"You want to live here, in Rocky Falls?" she asked, searching his face.

Julian met her gaze. He did want to stay here and he didn't realize it until just this moment. He'd been working on plans for the restaurant ever since he'd seen the undeveloped land. But maybe Dee Ann didn't want to leave Galveston. "I think it would be a great place to raise children, don't you?"

"Children?" Her eyes misted over. "Oh, Julian..."

She was going to cry again.

He couldn't have that. "Are you still not convinced we can make a go of marriage?" He ran his hand along her thigh. She was wearing a voluminous sleep shirt and her nose was red. She looked adorable.

"It's just—"

Julian let his hand wander into eyebrow-raising territory.

And Dee Ann raised her eyebrows. "What are you doing?"

"Convincing you to marry me." His hand passed over her hip. She was wearing panties. He wished she wasn't. Maybe he'd do something about it.

"And how is this supposed to convince me?" She removed his hand as he tugged at the lace.

"I'm reminding you of our greatest area of compatibility," he said, and kissed her. *Wake up, little hormones. I know you're there.*

She was soft and warm and her skin was satiny smooth. He deepened the kiss and felt a stirring in his nether regions. *I meant* her *hormones,* he informed his enthusiastic libido.

She tore her mouth away. "Julian, are you sure about this?" Her breathing quickened and she looked sweetly vulnerable.

Yes, we're sure, screamed his hormones. "Yes, I'm sure," echoed Julian.

"I mean—last night, you didn't—"

"Last night..." He was going to have to be *very* convincing to make up for last night. "Last night, I was a noble fool. Can you forget last night?"

She fingered his buttonless shirt. "I don't think so."

"Let me get rid of this reminder." With a sudden movement, Julian shrugged out of his shirt, discovering at the same time that he was still wearing his shoes. How smooth. He kicked them off, wincing as he felt one fly across the room.

Dee Ann burst into laughter, diffusing the tension, but spoiling the mood.

Although Julian had never tried to convince a woman to marry him before, he instinctively knew this wasn't the way. He sat on the bed and stared across the room. "I have a feeling I just flunked my audition."

Still laughing, Dee Ann gasped, "What were you auditioning for?"

"The role as your husband. The plan was to overwhelm you with incredible sex and propose again during the afterglow."

He heard a garbled sound. "That's blunt."

Julian sighed. When it mattered most, he had all the finesse of a teenager.

"Julian?"

"Hmm?" Julian was sorting through possible approaches. There must be *some* way he could salvage this.

He felt something nudge him. Dee Ann's foot.

She drew it over his back, pressing her toes into a particularly ticklish area near his waist. "I suppose I could give you the part based on your past work, however, I don't, er, recall precise details of your past work."

Slowly, he turned and looked down at her. "Are you asking me to refresh your memory?" He caught her foot and ran his hands over her calf, much as he'd done with the coffee-cake batter.

"Would you like to?" Her blue eyes gleamed in invitation.

A second chance. What a woman.

"Very much." As he spoke, Julian felt unfamiliar emotions seize him. Making love was something to be enjoyed and savored so that all parties had a good time and were left with fond memories when the affair was over.

But this wasn't going to be an affair and as yet, Dee Ann had no memories, fond or otherwise.

But he did.

Releasing her foot, he traced the line of her jaw, wiping away lingering signs of tears.

"You'll have to direct me." She smiled and Julian relaxed.

This was going to be great.

For both of them.

"I suppose I should set the stage so you'll know your motivation," he began.

"I think I know it already." She ran a finger down his breastbone.

He caught her finger and brought it to his lips. "There's more."

"I needed more?" She looked him up and down in frank appraisal.

Ah, yes. It was times like these that made those countless crunches and curls at the gym worth it. He stretched out next to her and propped himself on one elbow. "You'd unfortunately overheard a comment from one of the wedding guests comparing you to Nikki."

"And the comment was...?"

"Highly inaccurate." He tried to kiss her, but she moved her head and his kiss landed on her ear. Not bad...he nipped the lobe. Ears had potential.

"And the comment was...?" she repeated.

He might as well tell her so they could move on to more interesting activities. "It was suggested that you were a prude. Which, I'm happy to report, is *not* true."

"And I proved it by throwing our clothes over the side of the boat, right?"

"Among other things," Julian murmured. He remembered her moonlight striptease. He'd *always* remember her moonlight striptease.

"Then, I suppose that's where we'd better start," she announced, and pushed away from him before he realized what she intended.

To his complete astonishment and obviously growing delight, she stood by the side of the bed, pulled off her sleep shirt and tossed it over his head to the floor beyond.

All she was wearing were the lacy panties he'd discovered before. They were completely transparent, so she might as well not be wearing them at all.

And soon she wasn't.

"How's that?" Looking down at him, she grinned. "You should see your face."

Julian was trying to remember to breathe, just as he'd done that night on the *Honey Bee*.

"You're beautiful," he gasped. Completely inadequate words, then and now. That night, moonlight had silvered her skin. This morning, the sunlight filtering through peach-colored curtains gilded it.

And all he could do was stare, just as he'd stared that night.

She walked toward him, just as she had then, too. "Is this what I did next?" She crawled onto the bed and unfastened his belt.

"Yes." His voice was hoarse. He cleared his throat. "Except there was more kissing going on."

"Then by all means, let's have more kissing," she whispered and pressed close to him.

Julian cupped her face with his hands and kissed each eyelid, her nose and then her lips.

When he felt her hands at his waist, he smiled against her mouth.

"I did this before, right?" she asked.

"Oh, yes. How do you think I lost my wallet?"

Giggling, she peeled his pants and briefs off together, still trying to kiss him. She eventually had to use her foot to drag them around his ankles.

"Now what?" she asked and looked down.

"To hasten things along, I slipped my feet out." He proceeded to do so and reached for her.

Wearing a look of glee, Dee Ann ducked under his

arms, scrambled off the bed with his pants and threw them.

"Is that what I did?"

"Close enough. Though I wasn't terribly concerned with clothes at that point." And he wasn't terribly concerned with them at this point either. Julian followed her and swept her into his arms. "Then I carried you."

"You carried me all the way to the cabin?" she asked skeptically. "But it's down those tiny stairs."

She *would* remember those stairs and spoil the image. "Well, I'm carrying you now."

He'd twirled her around the cabin until they'd both collapsed on the berth in laughter, which had quickly become something else.

Now he set her down gently, treating her as though she might break.

"I *will* make you happy," he promised as his hand skimmed over her abdomen and lingered.

"Not there, you won't," she whispered and urged his hand lower.

As Julian settled against her, he savored the feel of her body, the scent of her skin and the taste of her mouth.

He was excited by her touch and the little sounds she made when he pleased her.

"Juuuuliaaaan."

He adored the way she said his name, wrapping it around him. "You like being kissed there?" he murmured and kissed her again.

"I like being kissed everywhere."

"Yes, I know."

She pulled back to focus on his face. "You know first-hand?"

"Dee Ann, dearest," he informed her with a lazy smile, "I didn't use my hand."

She matched his smile. "Perhaps it's time I used mine."

He inhaled sharply as one of her hands caressed him and the other drew his head to her breast. He circled it with his tongue and smiled up at her. "You taste just as good without the coffee-cake batter."

"We had to stop that day," she murmured, her eyes closed, her lips curved. "Now we don't."

Julian began weaving a special magic for them both, moving with a slow precision until he felt an insistent tug. "Dee Ann, it isn't nearly time yet." He kissed a particularly sensitive area he'd discovered near her ribs. She couldn't possibly be ready. "We had quite a prelude on the *Honey Bee*."

"We may have had a prelude on the *Honey Bee*, but it's time for the finale now!" she ordered.

She was ready.

He loved being bossed around, loved the way she drew him to her and clamped her legs around him.

But nothing compared to the moment they joined together, sighing in unison. Julian took her mouth in a melting kiss and felt his soul fuse with hers. He'd always held a little of himself back at this instant, but now, with Dee Ann, he didn't.

He had a reputation as a fabulous lover, and he knew it was because he never became so lost in the moment that he was unaware of his partner and her needs at any specific time. Oh, he enjoyed himself, thoroughly, but he never completely gave of himself.

And now he knew that by holding back, he'd been missing something wonderful, something essential.

He was barely aware of Dee Ann convulsing around him, barely heard her cry his name just before hers was ripped from his throat. He forgot where he was and even who he was.

Countless moments later, the muscles of his arms quivered and he drew deep, shuddering breaths. "I never knew," he said in wonder.

"How could I have forgotten *that?*" Dee Ann murmured into his neck.

Julian laid his cheek on the top of her head. How would he ever be satisfied with anything less than he'd shared with her? "Are you glowing?" he asked softly, nuzzling the hollow of her throat.

"Steaming," she said on a sigh.

"Have I convinced you to marry me?"

"If I say no, will you try to convince me some more?"

"How about if you say yes, we'll celebrate?"

"I'm convinced," she said promptly. "Let's celebrate."

He kissed her forehead, thinking he was a supremely lucky man.

"That's not much of a celebration," Dee Ann said.

He chuckled and rolled to his side, drawing her close. "We have to let the smoke clear before we can launch more fireworks."

She grinned. "Hurry up. *My* fuse is lit."

Those pregnancy hormones were really something.

"I hope it stays lit after the baby's born. I've heard some pretty sad tales."

"So have I. But we won't have to worry about that for a while, yet." She sighed. "What do you think of a fall wedding, say, November? Or should we wait until after the holidays? January?"

"You want to wait that long?" The time from their wedding until the birth of their child would already be short enough to raise eyebrows.

"I know it seems silly, but after being jilted, there's a part of me that wants to march down that aisle and make everyone forget about last spring. And, don't be jealous, but I want Carter to be your best man and I want him standing there this time."

"Can't we still do that, only a lot quicker?"

"But, Julian, it takes time to plan a wedding. I should know. And now that I think about it, November is far too early. It'll have to be January."

He ran a hand through his hair. "I don't know quite how to say this, since you're obviously, and surprisingly, unconcerned, but I would find it somewhat embarrassing to be marrying a visibly pregnant bride."

She blinked. "But, Julian, I'm not pregnant."

12

DEE ANN FELT Julian tense. "What do you mean, you're not pregnant?" he asked. His words were like a dark cloud threatening to smother their sunny future.

"The test was negative." It was sitting on the nightstand, right out in the open, plain as anything. How could he have missed it?

"Negative? You're sure?"

She nodded.

He sat up and felt for the plastic wand. "Negative," he repeated in a flat voice.

He sounded disappointed. He actually sounded disappointed. Dee Ann hadn't thought it possible to be any happier than she already was. This meant that Julian really and truly was committed to marriage and family. She snuggled closer.

"But you were crying," he said.

"Of course I was crying. I thought I'd never see you again."

"And you aren't going to have a baby." He seemed stuck on that point.

Dee Ann supposed it was because after resisting marriage and fatherhood for so long, he'd not only become accustomed to the idea, he was looking forward to it. "Well, not as soon as we thought, but, on the other hand—" she slipped her arms around his waist "—after this morning, who knows?"

Julian stared at her. "Oh, God."

"What?" She sat up.

"You weren't pregnant."

"Don't be disappointed. Think of all the fun we'll have—"

He cut her off. "You let me make love to you without taking *any* precautions."

"You didn't last time," she said with irritation.

"And we just spent two weeks in purgatory because of it!"

Where was the man who'd just made such wonderful love to her? Dee Ann drew the sheet up. "But it's different now. We're getting married."

"Marriage." His face froze over. "Of course." His eyes closed and his jaw clenched.

"Julian?"

When he opened his eyes, she caught her breath. They were as hard and cold as steel.

"That's what you've wanted all along, isn't it?"

"You *knew* that." And she knew something was terribly wrong.

"I knew it and I still allowed myself to get trapped." He stared straight ahead.

"There was no *trap*, Julian."

"You let me think you were pregnant."

"I *didn't!* You just assumed."

But Julian wasn't going to listen to her. "How could I have forgotten that you're the woman who was engineering a takeover of Belden Industries to occur *while you were on your honeymoon with the owner.*"

Her face heated. Yes, she had. It sounded cold, but the circumstances were different. Carter didn't love her and she didn't love him. She'd needed the security of knowing he'd remain in the marriage and not abandon her for some trophy wife after twenty years and a couple of kids.

"You're just as manipulative as you ever were." Julian threw off the covers and strode across the room to his clothes.

Even in the midst of their argument, Dee Ann could appreciate his long, lean form. "*You're* the one who immediately insisted on marriage. I wouldn't even discuss it with you until I'd taken the test."

"Because you know me and the kind of man I am. You knew I'd offer marriage."

"I even turned you down!"

He zipped up his pants. "I didn't say you weren't good."

Her mouth dropped open. "What is the *matter* with you? A few minutes ago you were talking about building a restaurant and a theater. What happened to all the plans to renovate Rocky Falls?" Her voice rose. "You said it was a good place to raise children!"

"That's when I thought I was having children." He sat on the wicker rocking chair and pulled on his socks.

"But we can still have children."

"You don't get it, do you?" He stood and slipped into his shoes. "I want to do things when *I*—" he jabbed his chest for emphasis "—want to do them. Not when they're dictated by circumstances."

"So we'll wait a while to have children."

He grabbed his torn shirt and stalked over to the bed. "But you can no longer assure me of that, can you?"

His was the face of a stranger. Dee Ann looked away.

"We had a reprieve," he continued, his voice hard. "We had a chance to go back to the way things were."

"But I thought..." *Thought you wanted children. Thought you wanted to marry me. Thought you wanted to build a life with me.*

Thought you loved me.

But love hadn't been mentioned by either of them and Dee Ann would rip out her tongue before admitting to Julian that she loved him now.

"Thought what?" he asked. "Thought I'd be thrilled to have my whole life turned upside down so you could live out an Ozzie-and-Harriet fantasy?"

"Get out." She pointed to the door. "Get out of this room and get out of this house. Go back to Galveston and your precious life with your penthouse and your wine collection."

"I intend to." He spun on his heel. "But I'll be back with another test."

"Don't bother. It won't make the slightest difference one way or the other."

He paused at the door. "Oh, yes, it will. If you're carrying my child, then we'll get married."

She couldn't let him stand there and dictate terms to

her without a response. "I wouldn't dream of inflicting you as a father on any child."

His gaze raked over her. "Not *any* child," he said. "*My* child."

IT WAS NOON before Dee Ann remembered the coffee shop and even then it was only after a concerned call from Adelaide.

Dee Ann went through the motions of making sandwiches, telling Adelaide that she wasn't feeling well.

"Honey, eat some soda crackers and it'll settle your stomach." Adelaide reached for a box from the pantry shelf.

"Thanks, but I'm not hungry," Dee Ann responded and tried to dredge up a smile.

"Of course you're not, but it'll pass." Adelaide handed her a plate of crackers. "And you've got to keep your strength up. Think of the baby."

Baby. Tears welled up in Dee Ann's eyes. Adelaide thought she was pregnant.

"Oh, honey." Adelaide enveloped her in a cinnamon-scented hug. "What does your young man say?"

Dee Ann tried to tell her she wasn't going to have a baby, but all she could do was cry. Her "young man" was gone.

Adelaide crooned sympathetically as Dee Ann sobbed.

She was still sobbing when Katrina, Louise and Brigitte found them.

"What's all this?" Katrina said. "It looks like I'm back just in time."

"Oh, Grandmother!" Dee Ann left one pair of ample arms for another.

"What's wrong, sweet child?" her grandmother asked.

"My Tony sold her young man a baby kit," announced Adelaide before Dee Ann could say anything.

A collective "ah" told Dee Ann that she'd better set them straight. But how could she explain that while this test was negative, she would have to take another?

"I left you alone in my house. I blame myself," Katrina said.

"Oh, no." Dee Ann pulled away. Her back was hurting from bending over the tiny woman. "You don't understand."

"I understand that you are crying your eyes out and I don't see Mr. Wainright. Where is he?"

Dee Ann took a deep breath. "I am *not* going to have a baby" *she hoped* "and Mr. Wainright has returned to Galveston."

She got all the way to the word *Galveston* before bursting into tears.

Dee Ann and the ladies moved to the kitchen table. Adelaide, apparently not trusting either modern science or hysterical denials, brought the crackers.

Haltingly, Dee Ann told them the entire story, omitting the fact that she'd probably be purchasing another home-test kit.

"And now he doesn't want to marry you?" Katrina asked when Dee Ann finished. "But he loves you!"

She shook her head, taking a tissue that one of the women offered. Julian didn't love her.

"I saw the way he looked at you." Katrina patted Dee

Ann's hand. "He's just scared of taking such a big step."

The other women murmured their agreement.

"And look what he did to the shop," Adelaide told her. "That was the act of a man who is in love."

"He'll be back," Katrina pronounced.

"SO, when are you going back?" Saunders asked after Julian relayed the tale of the devious Dee Ann Karrenbrock.

Julian was sorting through his mail. "A couple of weeks, unless I get a call from her telling me it isn't necessary." He didn't expect a call. He expected to track her down whether she was back in Galveston or had remained in Rocky Falls, and have it out with her face-to-face.

He dumped half his mail into the office wastebasket and nudged Saunders off the edge of his desk.

The lawyer poked at the pile of assorted papers cluttering Julian's in-box and withdrew a file folder. "These are the papers on that piece of land in Rocky Falls. What do you want done with them?"

Julian stared at the folder before taking it from Saunders. He'd wanted to buy the land for his restaurant. But that was when he'd expected to be living there.

"The owner's motivated. You could get a real good price."

With a look at Saunders, Julian tossed the folder back in the box.

Saunders shoved his hands into his pockets.

"If you're going to lecture me, get it over with," Julian grumbled.

"Was it just last weekend that I listened to you babble on for hours about the newest Hill Country tourist mecca?"

"Saunders, a true friend wouldn't remind me of that." Julian wished Saunders would go away.

"You're abandoning all your ideas? Your plans? What happened?"

"I refuse to be trapped by a conniving female, that's what!" Julian stood. "Did you finish the title search on—"

"But you could still develop the property without being married to Dee Ann," Saunders interrupted as if Julian hadn't spoken.

Julian exhaled in exasperation. "But I just *might* be married to her."

"In that case, you'll be developing Rocky Falls?"

"I—I..." Julian sank into his leather chair and rubbed his temple.

Saunders planted both fists on the desk and leaned forward. "You know what? I *like* Dee Ann. And I think you feel a lot more than that for her."

"Try hate."

"Try love."

The word hung between them. Saunders grinned a huge wolflike grin. "You love her and you're scared. Admit it."

"You're nuts."

"Am I?" Saunders stood, his expression smug. "Then

tell me why she's in the same condition she was two weeks ago, hmm?"

"Because I thought she was already pregnant!" he snapped. Not that it was any of Saunders's business.

"Is that what she told you?"

"No." Julian looked away.

"You *wanted* her to be pregnant so you'd be 'forced'—" Saunders curved his fingers in quote marks, which he knew full well irritated Julian "—to marry her."

"That's ridiculous."

"No, I've hit it on the money. You love her and you're scared."

"I'm not!"

"Julian's in love." Saunders chortled. "Oh, the mighty bachelor has fallen."

"Isn't there somebody you can go sue?"

"What a good idea." Saunders beamed and headed for the door. "I'll call Dee Ann and see if she wants to retain my services."

"That's conflict of interest!" Julian shouted as the lawyer disappeared down the hall.

"So sue me!" Saunders shouted back.

"THERE'S A CUSTOMER at the coffee bar," Katrina told Dee Ann. "And he wants cappuccino."

Dee Ann nodded. Her grandmother refused to learn how to work the cappuccino machine. And why should she? She had declared her coffee-shop days over in no uncertain terms.

Dee Ann believed her. There was no reason for her to

keep the shop open and she couldn't really say why she did anymore. She hadn't listed it with a commercial Realtor, either. She'd done nothing but wake up at five o'clock each morning and work until she dropped and then did it all again.

Her grandmother would wander in from time to time and cluck at her, but Dee Ann didn't know what else to do with her life.

She didn't want to go back to her father's company.

She didn't even want to return to Galveston.

Maybe she'd just stay right here and run KK's Koffee Shoppe forever.

Wiping her hands on a towel, she pushed open the swinging door to the dining area and stopped.

Julian sat at the counter.

Their eyes met.

"Get your own cappuccino," Dee Ann said by way of greeting. Then she turned around and went back into the kitchen.

She would have continued walking right out the back door, but her grandmother stopped her.

"Dee Ann, talk to him."

"I have nothing to say."

"But you love him."

"He knows and it makes no difference."

"You have told him that you love him? This I cannot believe."

Dee Ann hadn't actually said the words, but Julian could figure it out. Besides, she wasn't planning to continue loving him. She'd get over it like any other illness.

And there was the germ now, standing in the doorway.

"Now you two can talk," her grandmother said.

"I have nothing to say to this man," Dee Ann stated and looked him right in the eye.

Katrina clucked. "Yes, you do. And I will leave you two alone, but before I do, could I borrow Mr. Wainright?"

"You can *have* Mr. Wainright."

"How may I be of service?" Julian asked in his liquid voice, making Dee Ann appear churlish.

Katrina opened the kitchen door. "My potatoes are in the cellar out back here."

"Grandmother, I told you I'd bring up those potatoes for you," Dee Ann protested.

"But the sack is so heavy." The older woman's forehead wrinkled.

"Allow me," Julian offered as Dee Ann knew he would.

Katrina unhooked the wooden cellar door and pulled open the gray plywood to reveal steps.

Dee Ann hated going into the cellar and grudgingly admitted to herself that she was glad she didn't have to do so now. At least Julian was good for something.

He stepped inside and felt for the handrail. "Is there a light switch?"

"There on the right," Katrina directed.

They could hear him flipping the switch. "The light bulb seems to be burnt out. But if you two stand back from the door, maybe there'll be enough light for me to see."

Dee Ann gladly stood back while Katrina stepped inside the kitchen.

"What size sack are we talking about?" Julian's voice sounded muffled.

Dee Ann shivered.

"Fifty pounds," Katrina called. She thrust a flashlight into Dee Ann's hands. "Go take this to him."

"Down there?" Dee Ann recoiled.

"Yes." Katrina pushed her toward the door. "Dee Ann is coming with a flashlight, Mr. Wainright."

Dee Ann stepped over the threshold. "Come to the bottom of the stairs and I'll toss it to you," she said into the darkness.

"I can't see. You're blocking the light," he grumbled.

"Go," her grandmother urged. "Take it to him. He might drop the flashlight and break it."

Dee Ann climbed down no more than five steps before the door slammed shut. She screamed and dropped the flashlight.

A second later, she heard a sickening thud and Julian's muffled curses, followed by a larger thud.

"Julian!"

"I'm alive," she heard, but it wasn't very convincing.

"Are you all right?" Holding the handrail, Dee Ann felt her way down the rest of the stairs. "Where are you?"

"Right he—*oof*," he said at the same moment Dee Ann's foot struck him and she tripped.

Clawing at the blackness, she braced herself to hit the hard, dirt floor, landing on solid, warm Julian instead.

"Julian!" she shrieked as he wrapped his arms around her.

"Yes, and that was my ear."

She lowered her voice and struggled to get off him. "Where did the flashlight hit you?"

"My foot. You don't have to move, you know."

"But I'm on top of you."

"As I said, you don't have to move, except for the wiggling. That's kind of nice."

What was her grandmother thinking to lock her down here with this maniac? Dee Ann held herself rigid. "I want you to know that I had nothing at all to do with this."

She heard a sigh. "I know. I did."

"You told my grandmother to lock us in the cellar?"

"Actually, it was her idea when I told her that you wouldn't speak to me."

"That's because I have nothing to say to you."

"Fine, but I have a few things to say to you."

"I'm not going to listen." She squirmed as she tried to free herself. Julian tightened his arms around her.

She could feel his smile. She could feel other things, as well. "Is that a pregnancy kit in your pocket, or are you just glad to see me?"

"I'm just glad to see you." He moved his hands over her hips and pressed her against him. "Real glad."

Dee Ann gasped. "Stop that!"

"Keep talking so I can find your mouth."

"Let me go."

"Thanks. That'll do."

She should have known she'd end up kissing him. He

was so *good* at it. He was good at virtually everything else, as well. But she didn't want to think about that. But if she didn't think about that, she'd think about being on the cellar floor with all the creepy-crawly things that were probably down here.

Hands on either side of her face, Julian lifted her mouth away from his.

"Don't stop. Spiders." She ducked her head.

Julian kissed her quickly, then chuckled. "We can't leave until we talk."

"Who needs talking? I didn't like the last time we talked."

"I know. Can you forgive me for saying those unforgivable things?"

"No." Dee Ann propped herself up with one hand and searched for the flashlight with the other. Something feathered over her fingers. Squealing, she snatched her hand back and huddled against his chest.

"My ears are ringing."

"Hurry up and say what you were going to say so we can get out of here!"

"Will you marry me?"

That wasn't what she'd been expecting. "You're slipping. You forgot to ask me to take a pregnancy test first."

"I'm not going to. Will you marry me?"

"No. Is that all?"

"I realize that this isn't the most romantic location for a proposal—"

"Romance has nothing to do with it."

"But I *am* sincere."

"So am I. The answer's no. Now, signal my grandmother to let us out of here." She tried to scramble off him.

"Not yet. Dee Ann, I bought the land next to the falls. I'm going to build my restaurant."

She wanted to say something nasty and hurtful, but she couldn't. "Congratulations, but we don't have to get married for you to build your restaurant. I'll behave civilly when we run into each other. Maybe I'll even eat there on occasion."

"I *want* us to be married."

Dee Ann closed her eyes, even though it was dark. Why was fate torturing her this way? "Julian, I'm not pregnant." And that should end the marriage discussion.

"Well...we could work on that." His hands toyed with the hem of her shirt.

"Not *here*."

"I'll let you stay on top?"

She sighed. "I realize you're only kidding, but it's not something I feel comfortable joking about anymore."

"I'm sorry." He stroked her back. "I know you want children."

"Yes, I do." Dee Ann rested her head on his chest and listened to his heartbeat, savoring the last few minutes of closeness. "But I want to raise them with a man who wants them as much as I do."

"Are we talking ten or twelve kids here?" Julian asked.

She laughed. "No, just two."

He was silent, though he continued tracing circles on her back. "I can handle two."

"Look, Julian, I'm not sure you're the one to join me in my—what did you call it?—Ozzie-and-Harriet fantasy."

He made a disgusted sound. "I said some awful things to you. But there's one thing I didn't say."

"What?"

"I love you."

She felt the words rumble from his body to hers and wondered if he meant them. "You hurt me. If you loved me, then why did you hurt me like that?"

He sighed, his breath fanning the top of her head. "I think I was afraid of my feelings," he admitted quietly. "When I made love to you that morning, there was a time when I lost myself and frankly, another person having that sort of power over me was terrifying. I was looking for an excuse to distance myself."

She tried to see his face. There was the barest sliver of light from the crack in the cellar door, but she couldn't make out Julian's features. "So when did you decide you loved me?"

"After I got back to Galveston. Saunders had to tell me."

That provoked Dee Ann into an unwilling laugh. "Couldn't you have figured it out for yourself?"

"I would have, eventually. He just saved me some time."

Dee Ann smiled. "I think I've become rather fond of Saunders."

"He has his moments, but he doesn't belong in this one."

"Be sure and invite him to the wedding."

"I hope that means there's going to be one. I do love you, Dee Ann." He pulled her down for one of his breath-stealing kisses.

"I love you, too." She sighed. "Uh, Julian?"

"Yes?"

"Is that your hand crawling up my leg?"

"No. Though if that's your wish—"

"Get me out of this cellar!"

Epilogue

Five years later

"YOU HIRED a circus for Alexandra's birthday?" Dee Ann stared as a baby elephant and his trainer roamed the Wainright Inn's grounds.

"Just a small one." Julian turned to the little boy in his arms. "You want to ride the elephant, John Henry?"

The toddler stuck his finger in his mouth.

"I want a ride, Daddy!" A blond-haired girl tugged insistently at Julian's pant legs.

He bent down until he was eye level with her. "Not only can you ride, you can be first because you're the birthday girl."

"Yeah!" Alexandra jumped and clapped her hands. "I want to ride now!"

"Well, then, let's go!"

Dee Ann chuckled and shook her head. "You're spoiling her, Julian."

He bent to kiss Dee Ann and the sleeping baby she held in her arms. "I love spoiling her. I love spoiling all of you."

And Dee Ann admitted that she loved being spoiled.

She watched as Julian led their daughter and older son across the park to the inn and the Rocky Falls Theater.

Yes, Julian Wainright, former bachelor, was a thoroughly domesticated husband.

And then she thought back to last night.

Domesticated, but not tamed.

The very best kind.